JOHNNY BOO

AND THE HAPPY APPLES

I'm going to eat ALL these apples while they Read the Story!

Don't forget to SHARE, Squiggle.

FOR ELI, OLIVER,
AND THOSE OTHER KIDS,
DECLAN & MARIPOSA.

ISBN 978-1-60309-041-4
1. Children's Books
2. Apples / Fruits & Vegetables
3. Graphic Novels

Johnny Boo and the Happy Apples © 2009 James
Kochalka. Published by Top Shelf Productions,
PO Box 1282, Marietta, GA 30061-1282, USA.
Publishers: Brett Warnock and Chris Staros.
Top Shelf Productions® and the Top Shelf
logo are registered trademarks of Top Shelf
Productions, Inc. All Rights Reserved. No part
of this publication may be reproduced without
permission, except for small excerpts for
purposes of review. Visit our online catalog at
www.topshelfcomix.com. First Printing,
August 2009. Printed in China.

CHAPTER ONE:

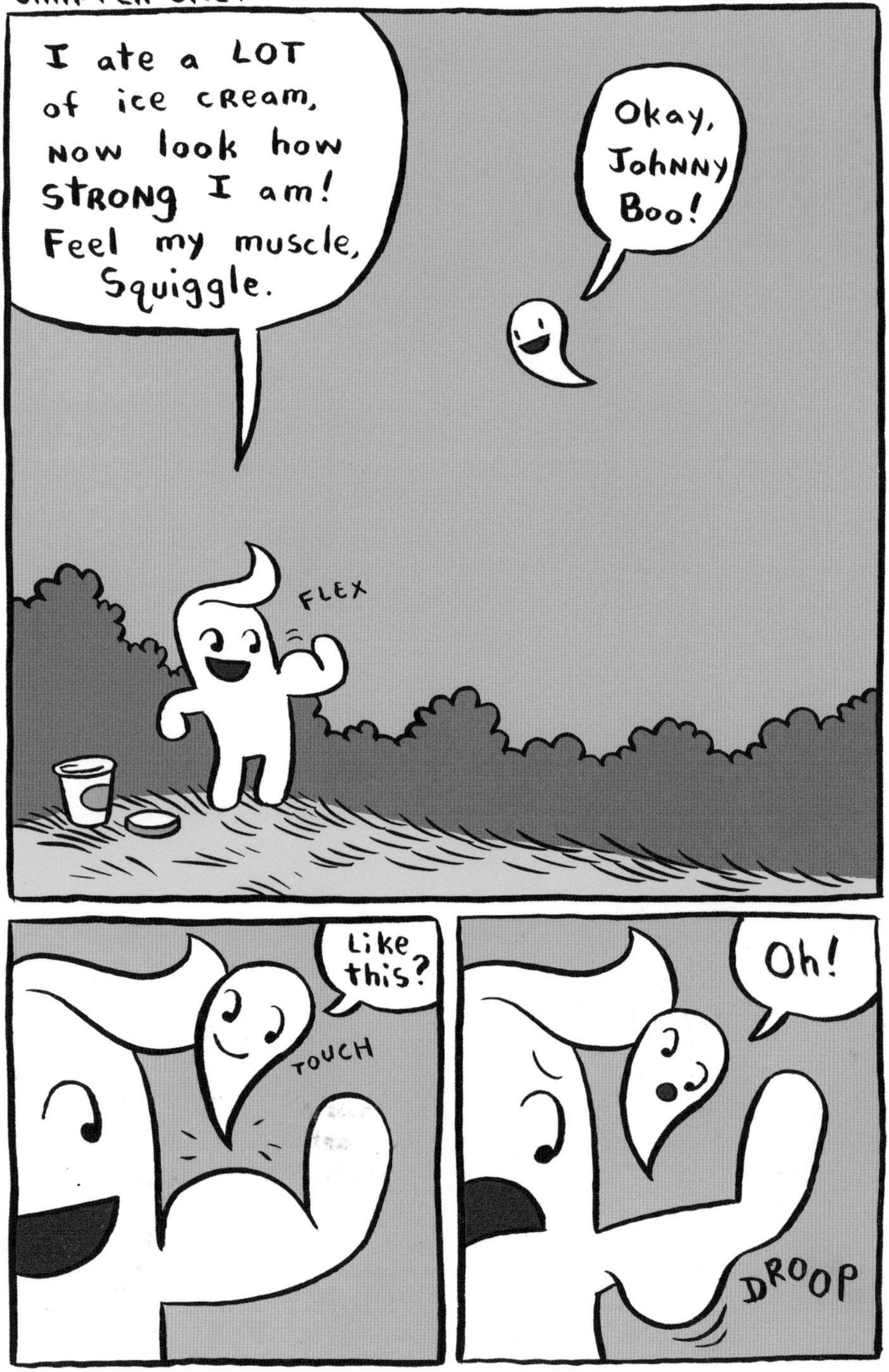
I ate a LOT of ice cream, now look how STRONG I am! Feel my muscle, Squiggle.
Okay, Johnny Boo!
FLEX
Like this?
TOUCH
Oh!
DROOP

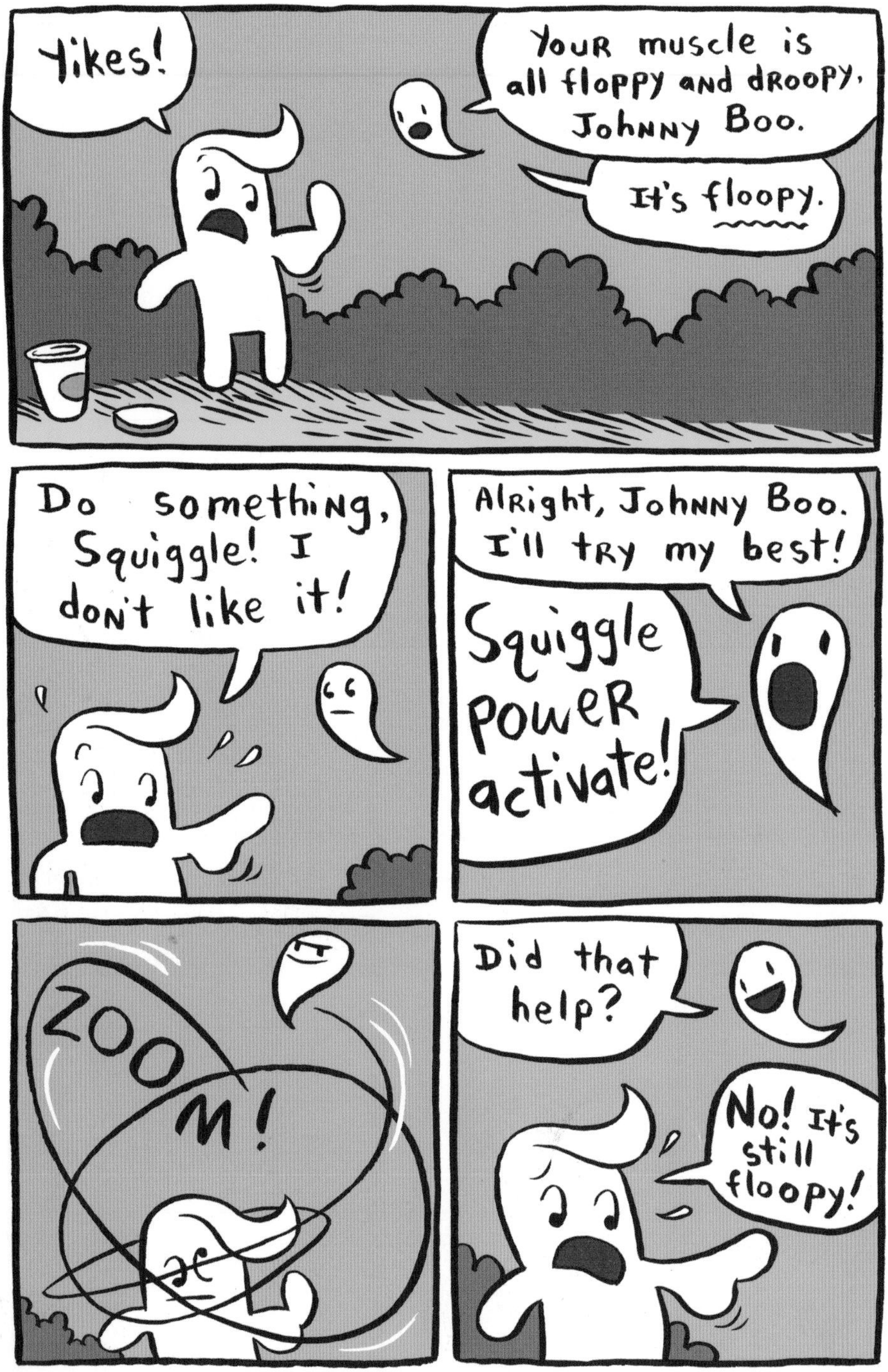
Yikes!
Your muscle is all floppy and droopy, Johnny Boo.
It's floopy.
Do something, Squiggle! I don't like it!
Alright, Johnny Boo. I'll try my best!
Squiggle power activate!
ZOOOM!
Did that help?
No! It's still floopy!

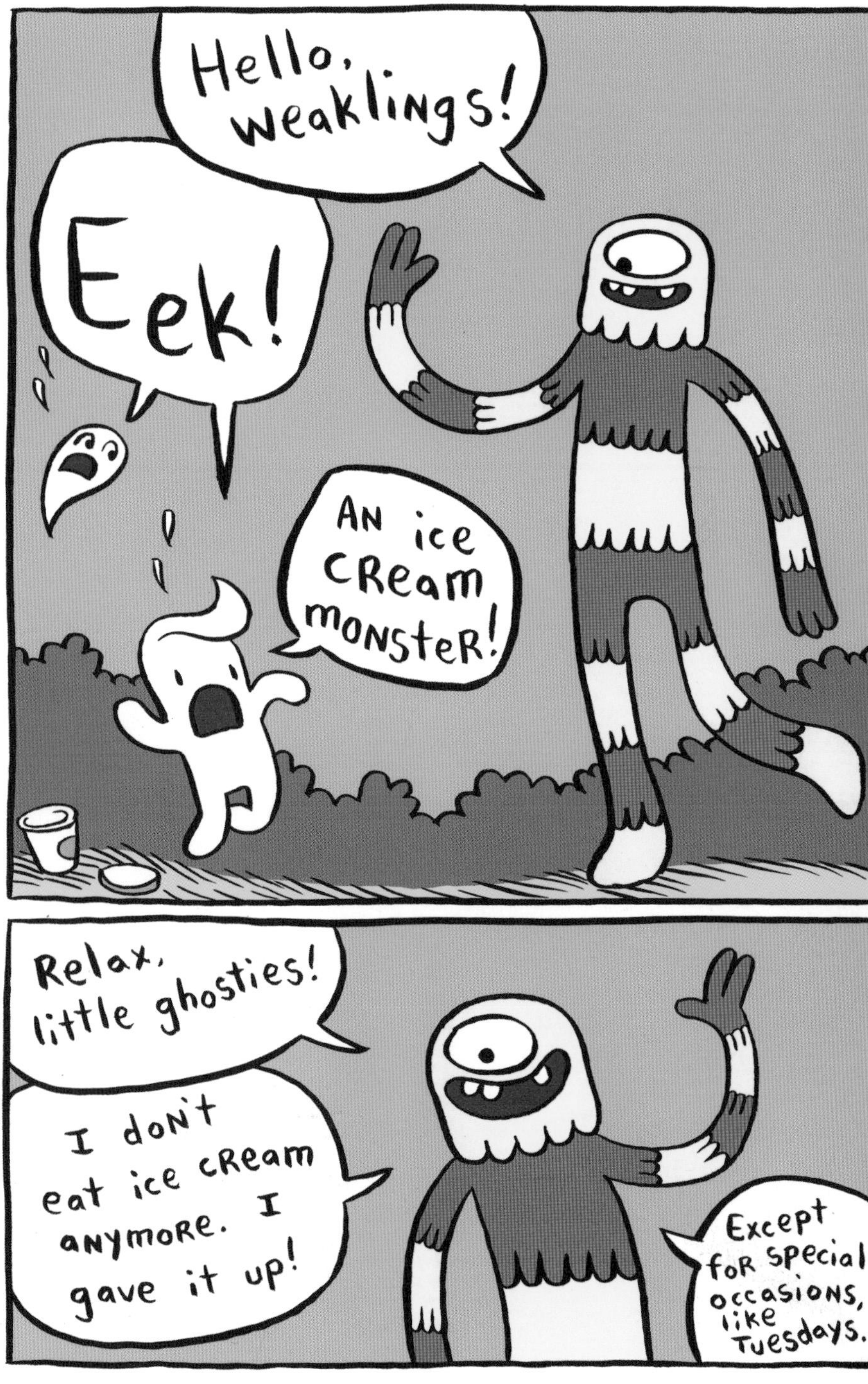
Hello, weaklings!
Eek!
AN ice CReam monsteR!
Relax, little ghosties!
I don't eat ice cReam anymoRe. I gave it up!
Except foR special occasions, like Tuesdays.

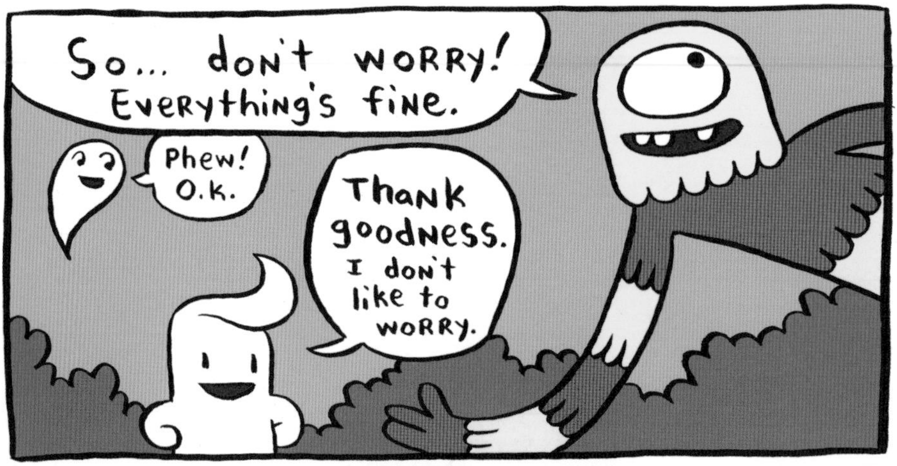
So... don't WORRY! Everything's fine.
Phew! O.K.
Thank goodness. I don't like to WORRY.

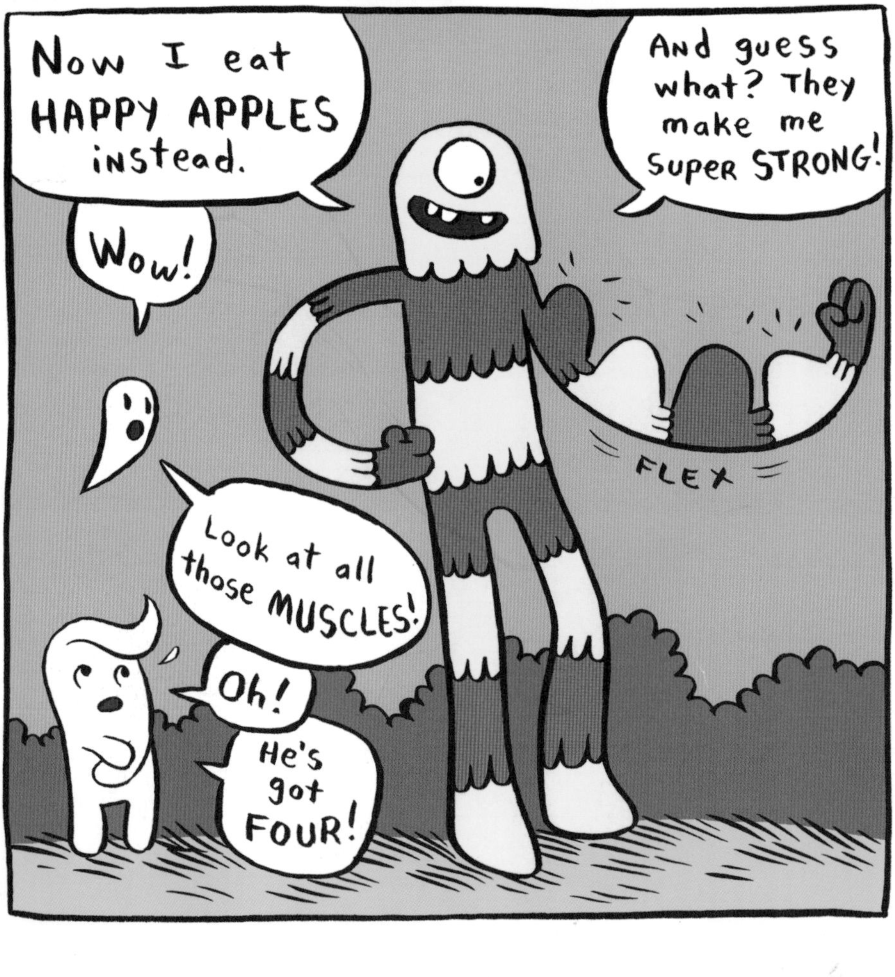
Now I eat HAPPY APPLES instead.
And guess what? They make me SUPER STRONG!
Wow!
FLEX
Look at all those MUSCLES!
Oh!
He's got FOUR!

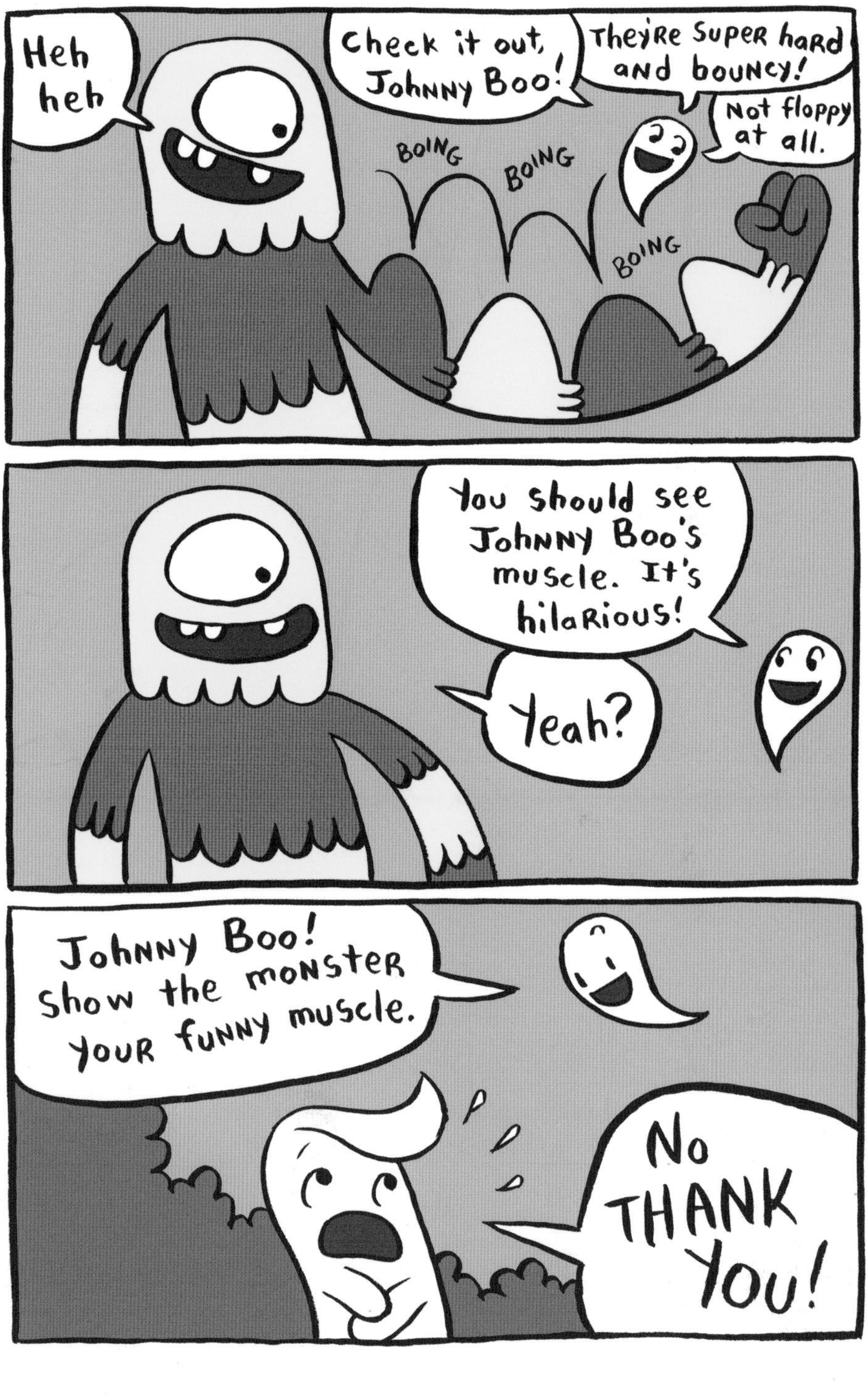
Heh heh
Check it out, Johnny Boo!
They're super hard and bouncy!
Not floppy at all.
BOING
BOING
BOING
You should see Johnny Boo's muscle. It's hilarious!
Yeah?
Johnny Boo! Show the monster your funny muscle.
No THANK YOU!

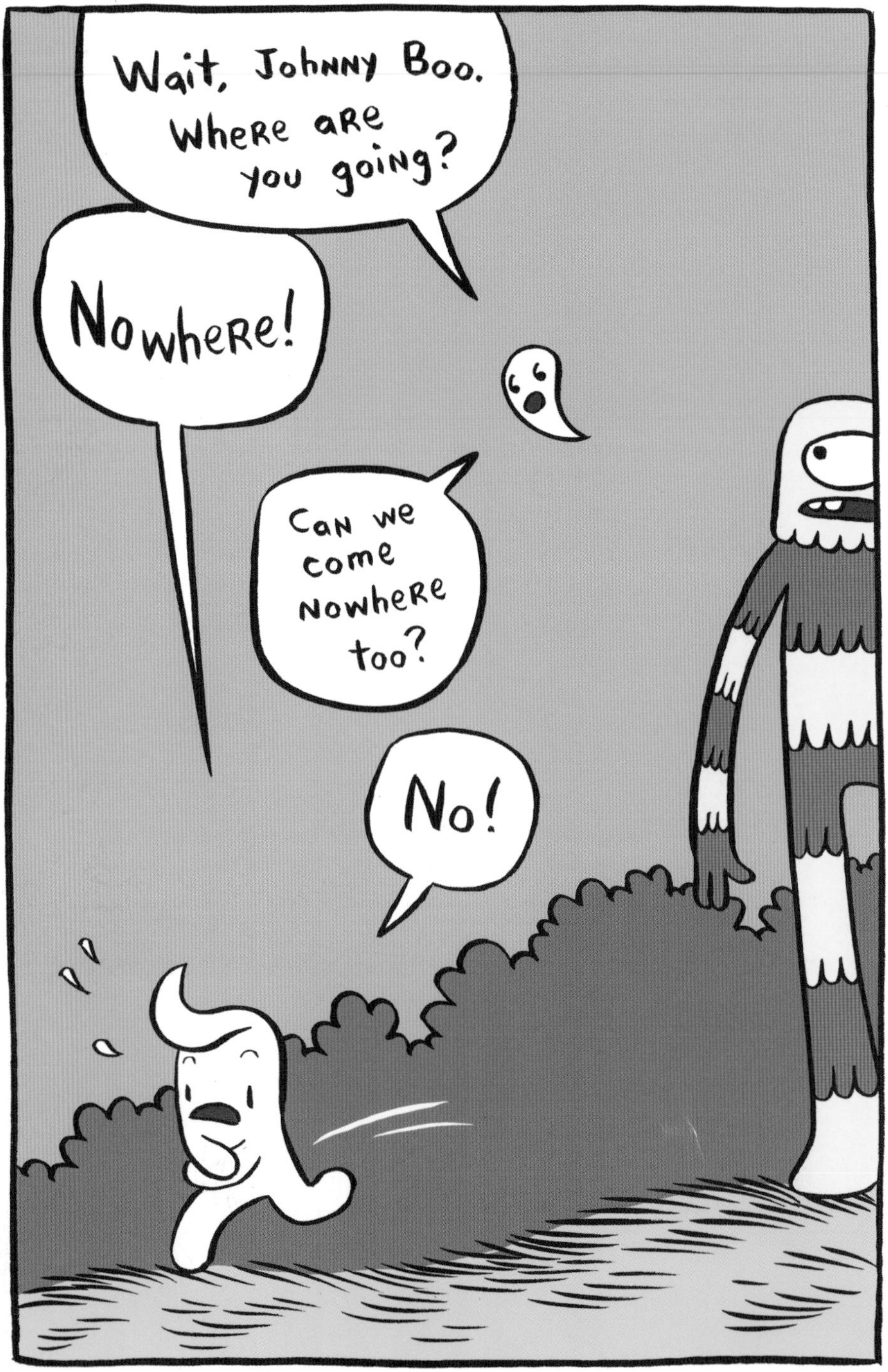
Wait, Johnny Boo. Where are you going?
Nowhere!
Can we come nowhere too?
No!

CHAPTER TWO:

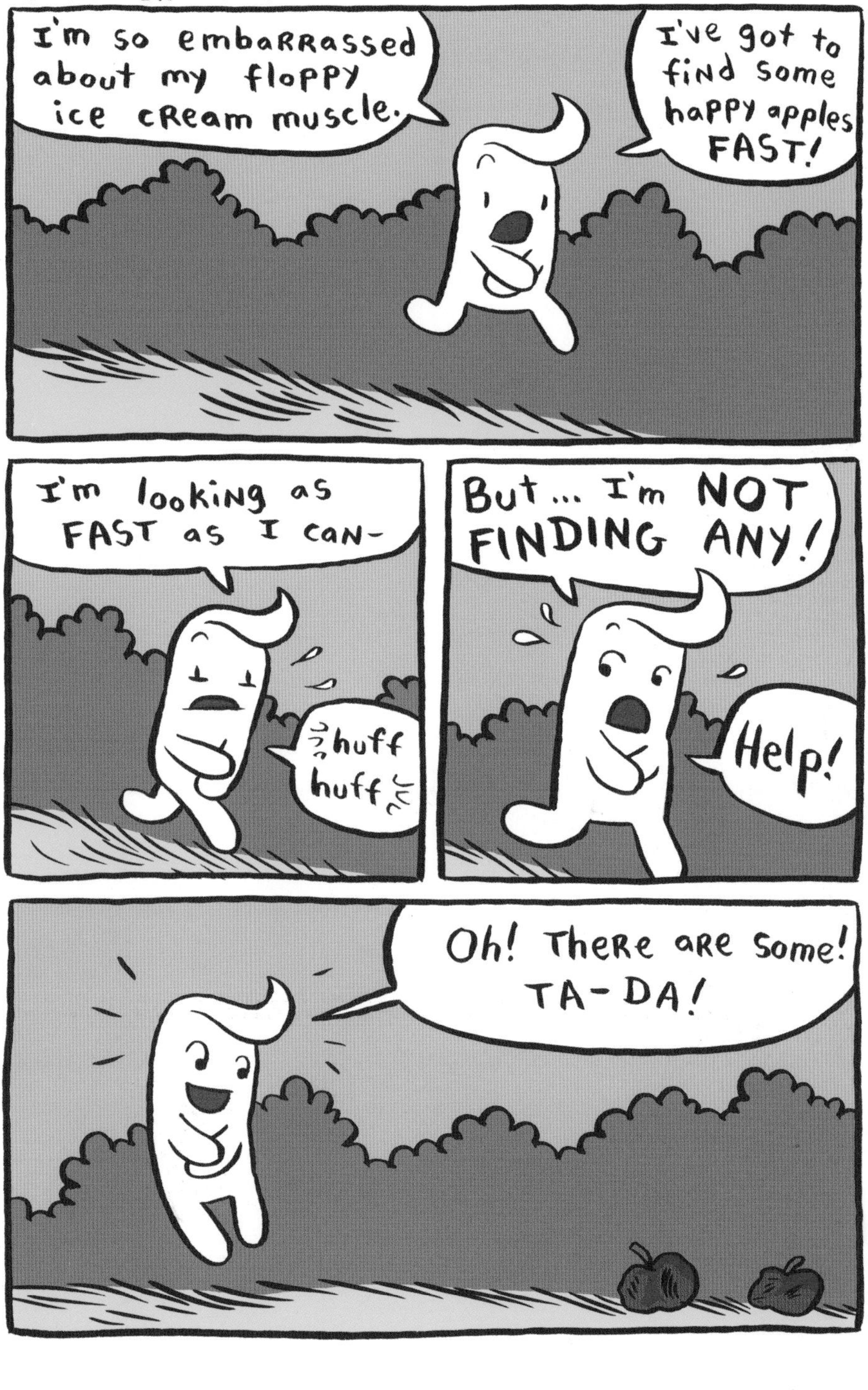
I'm so embarrassed about my floppy ice cream muscle.
I've got to find some happy apples FAST!
I'm looking as FAST as I can-
huff huff
But... I'm NOT FINDING ANY!
Help!
Oh! There are some! TA-DA!

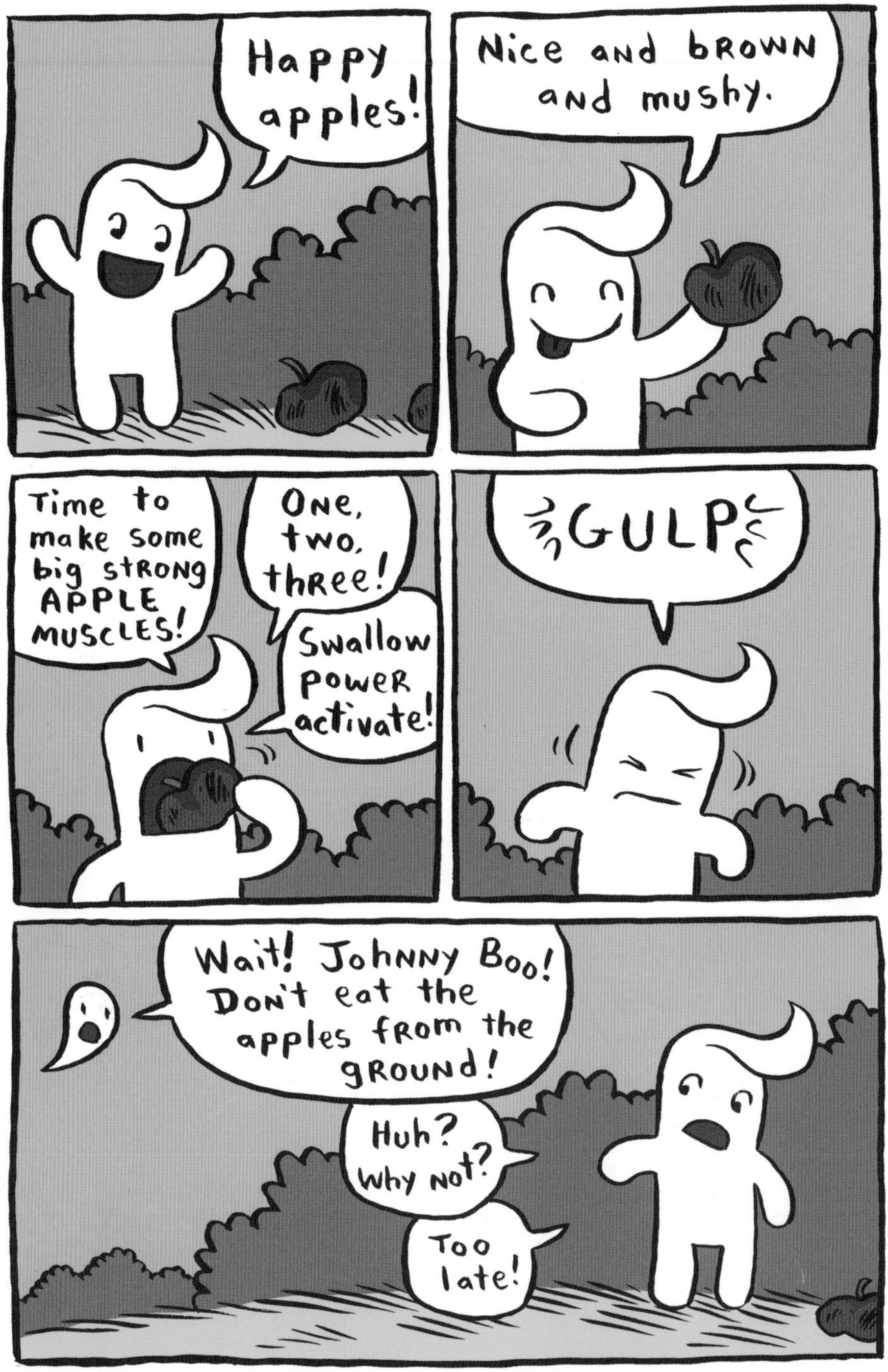
Happy apples!
Nice and BROWN and mushy.
Time to make some big STRONG APPLE MUSCLES!
ONE, two, three!
Swallow power activate!
GULP
Wait! Johnny Boo! Don't eat the apples from the ground!
Huh? Why not?
Too late!

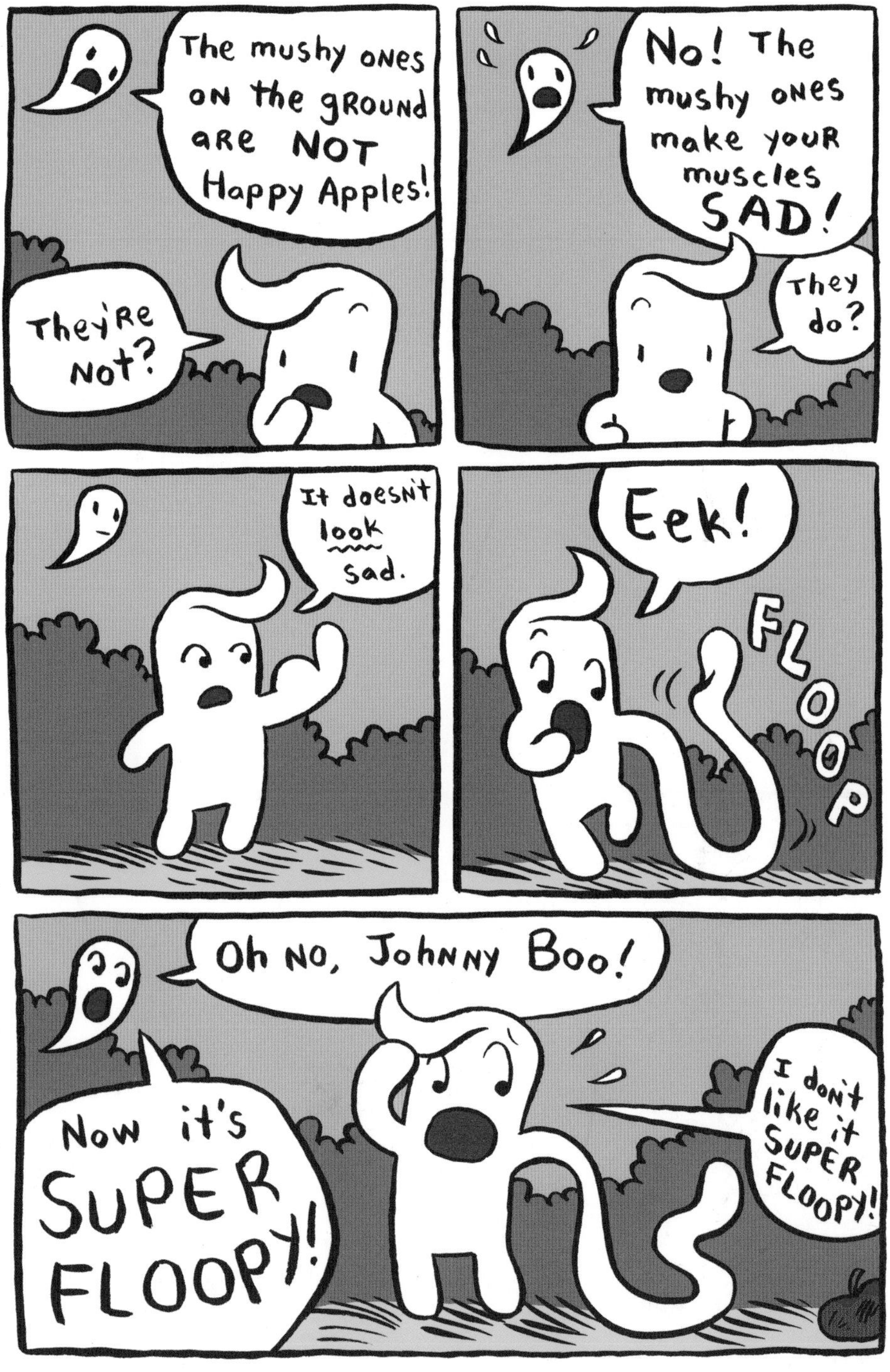
The mushy ones on the ground are NOT Happy Apples!
They're Not?
No! The mushy ones make your muscles SAD!
They do?
It doesn't look sad.
Eek!
FLOOP
Oh no, Johnny Boo!
Now it's SUPER FLOOPY!
I don't like it SUPER FLOOPY!

CHAPTER THREE:

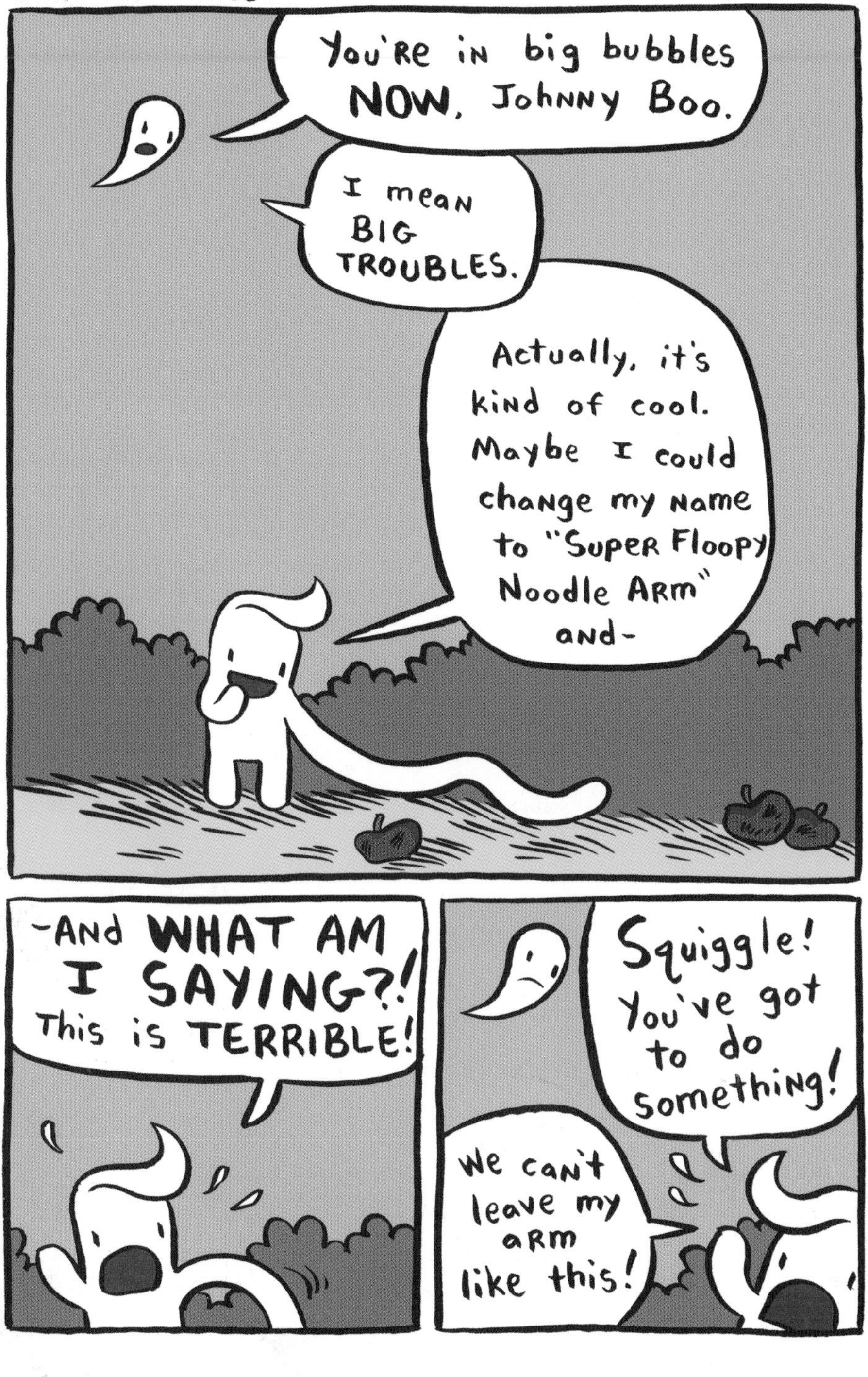

You're in big bubbles NOW, Johnny Boo.
I mean BIG TROUBLES.
Actually, it's kind of cool. Maybe I could change my name to "Super Floopy Noodle Arm" and-
-And WHAT AM I SAYING?! This is TERRIBLE!
Squiggle! You've got to do something!
We can't leave my arm like this!

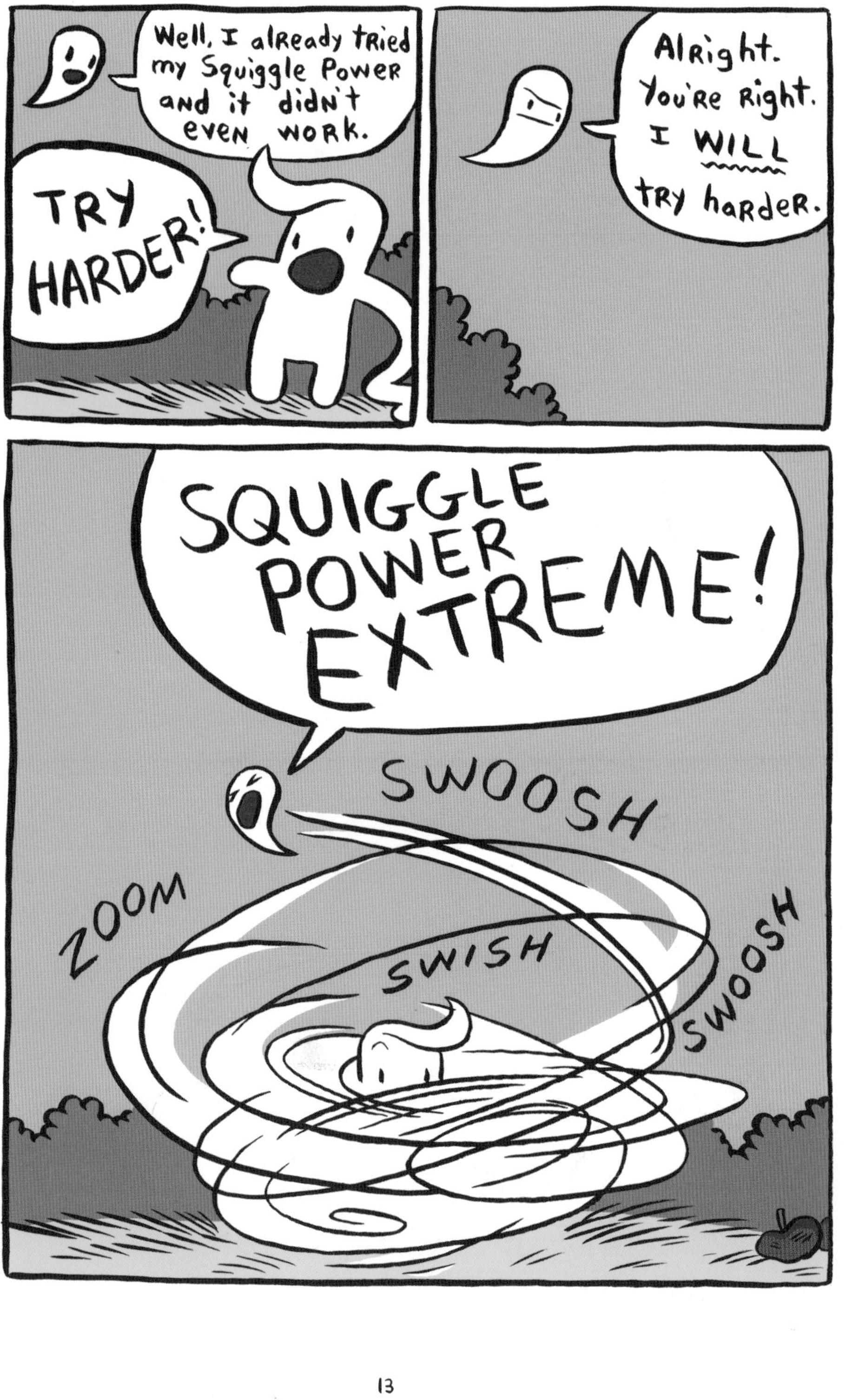
Well, I already tried my Squiggle Power and it didn't even work.
TRY HARDER!
Alright. You're right. I WILL try harder.
SQUIGGLE POWER EXTREME!
SWOOSH
ZOOM
SWISH
SWOOSH

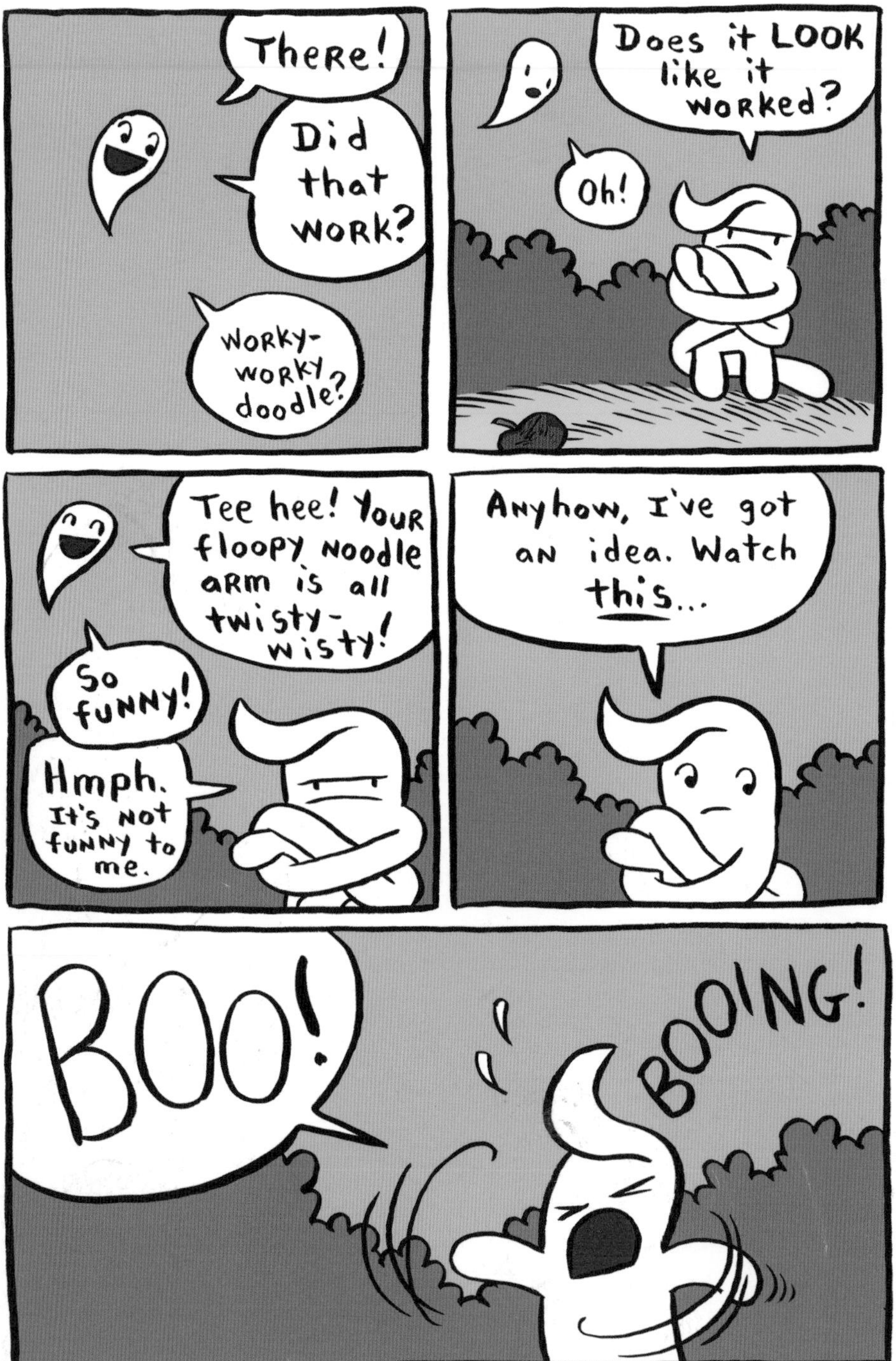
There!
Did that work?
Worky-worky doodle?
Does it LOOK like it worked?
Oh!
Tee hee! Your floopy noodle arm is all twisty-wisty!
So funny!
Hmph. It's not funny to me.
Anyhow, I've got an idea. Watch this...
BOO!
BOOING!

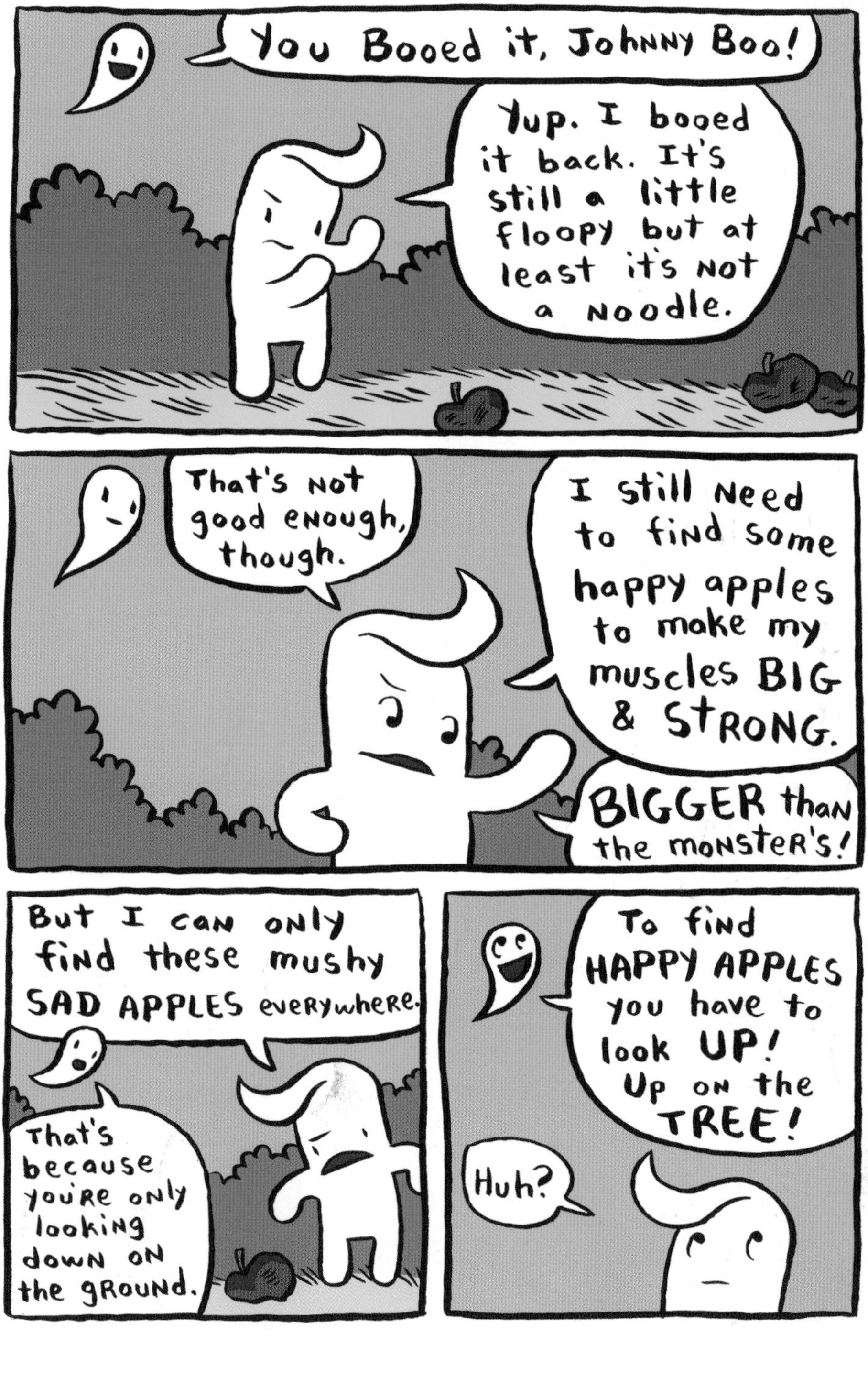
You Booed it, Johnny Boo!
Yup. I booed it back. It's still a little floopy but at least it's not a noodle.
That's not good enough, though.
I still need to find some happy apples to make my muscles BIG & STRONG.
BIGGER than the monster's!
But I can only find these mushy SAD APPLES everywhere.
That's because you're only looking down on the ground.
To find HAPPY APPLES you have to look UP! Up on the TREE!
Huh?

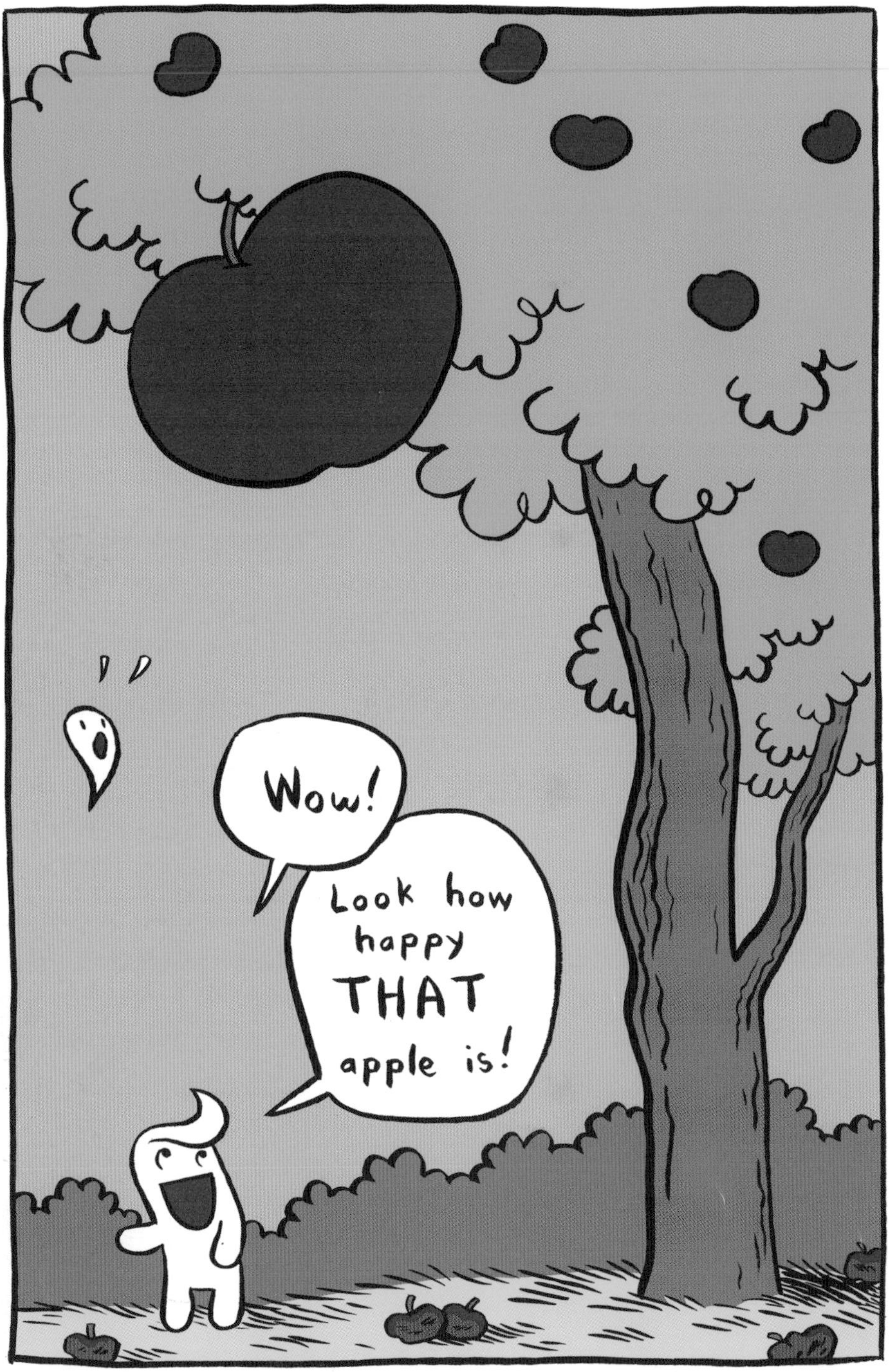
Wow!
Look how happy THAT apple is!

CHAPTER FOUR:

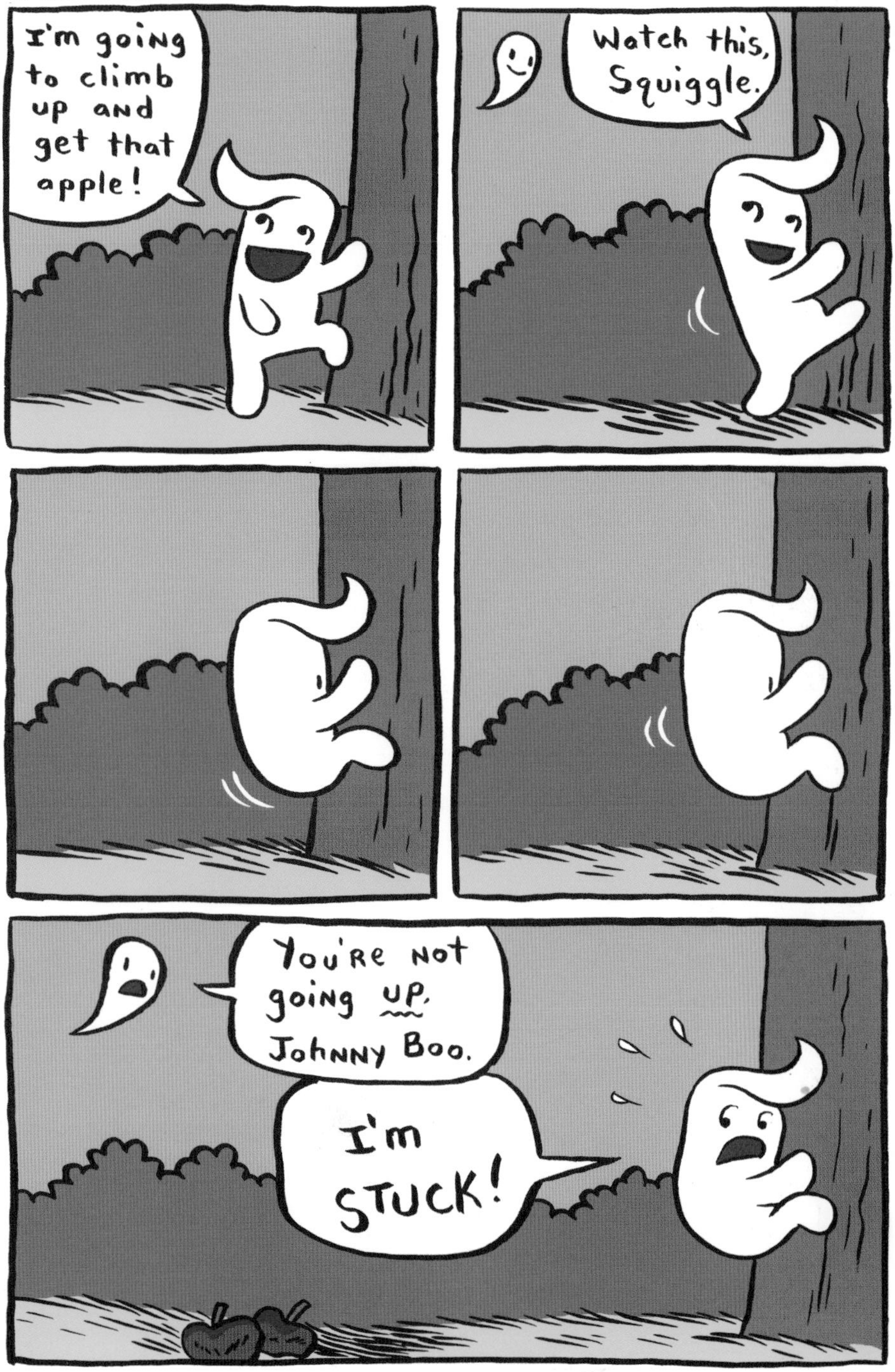
I'm going to climb up and get that apple!
Watch this, Squiggle.
You're not going UP, Johnny Boo.
I'm STUCK!

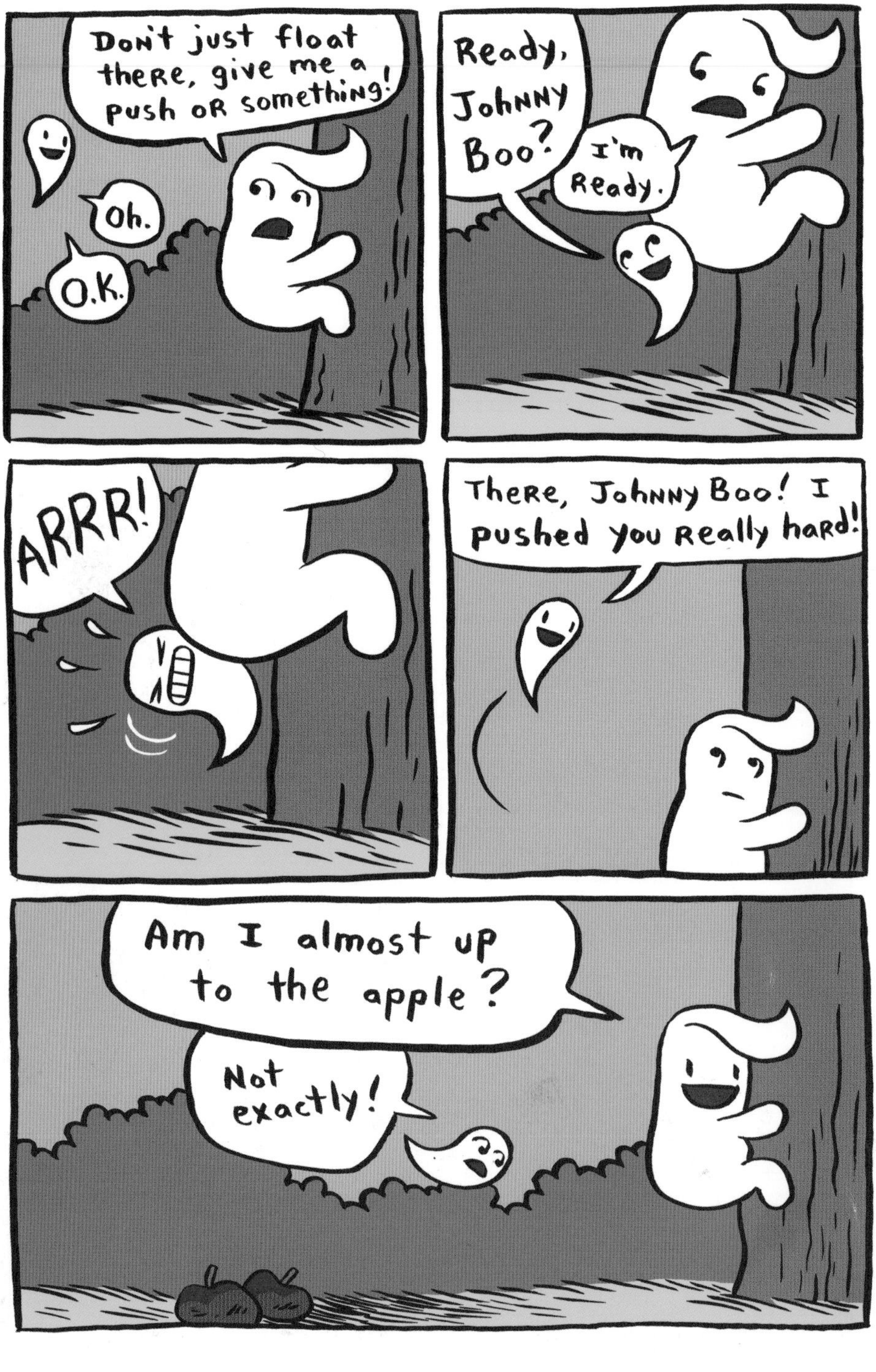
Don't just float there, give me a push or something!
Oh.
O.K.
Ready, Johnny Boo?
I'm Ready.
ARRR!
There, Johnny Boo! I pushed you really hard!
Am I almost up to the apple?
Not exactly!

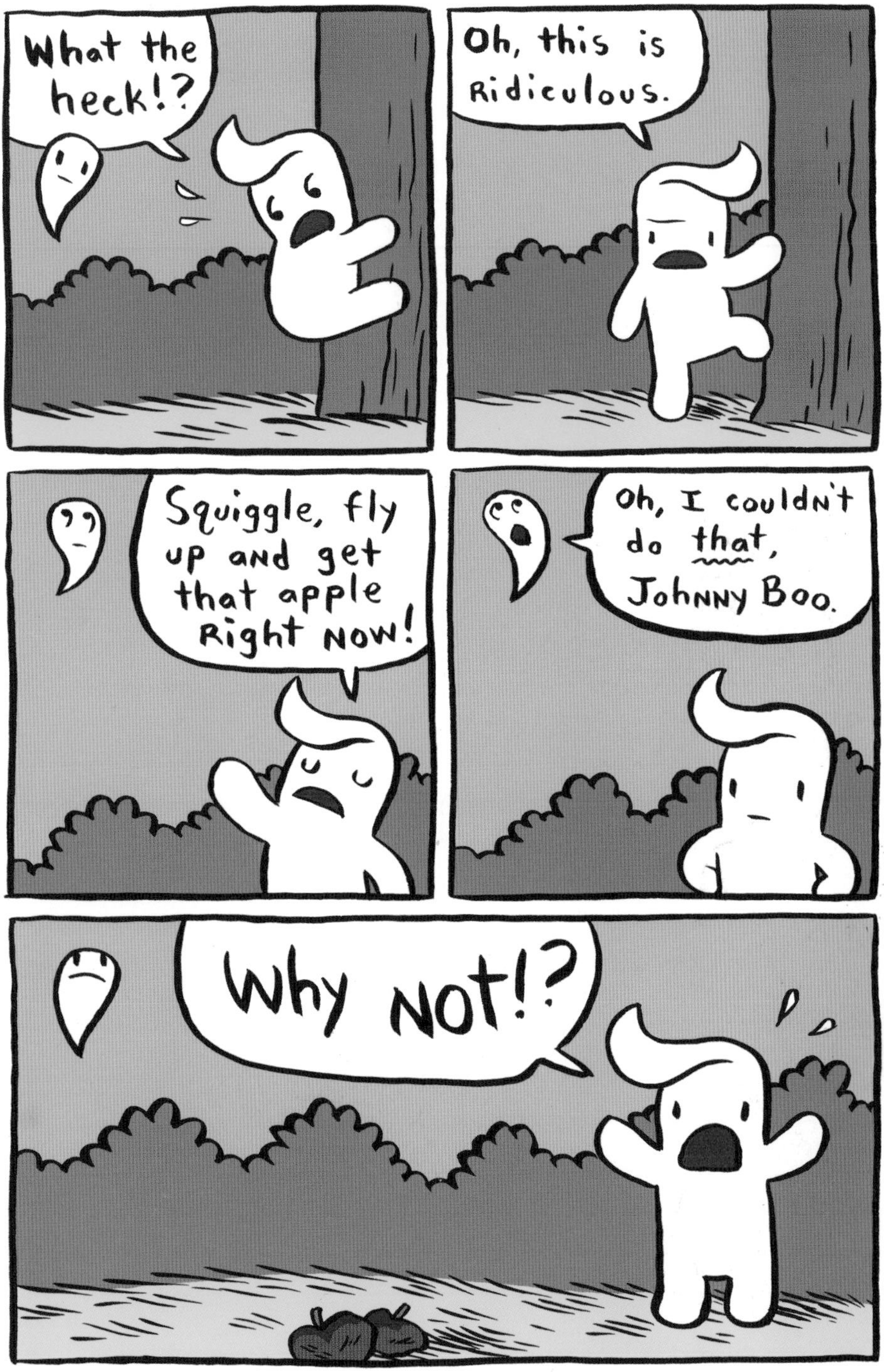
What the heck!?
Oh, this is Ridiculous.
Squiggle, fly up and get that apple Right Now!
Oh, I couldn't do that, Johnny Boo.
Why Not!?

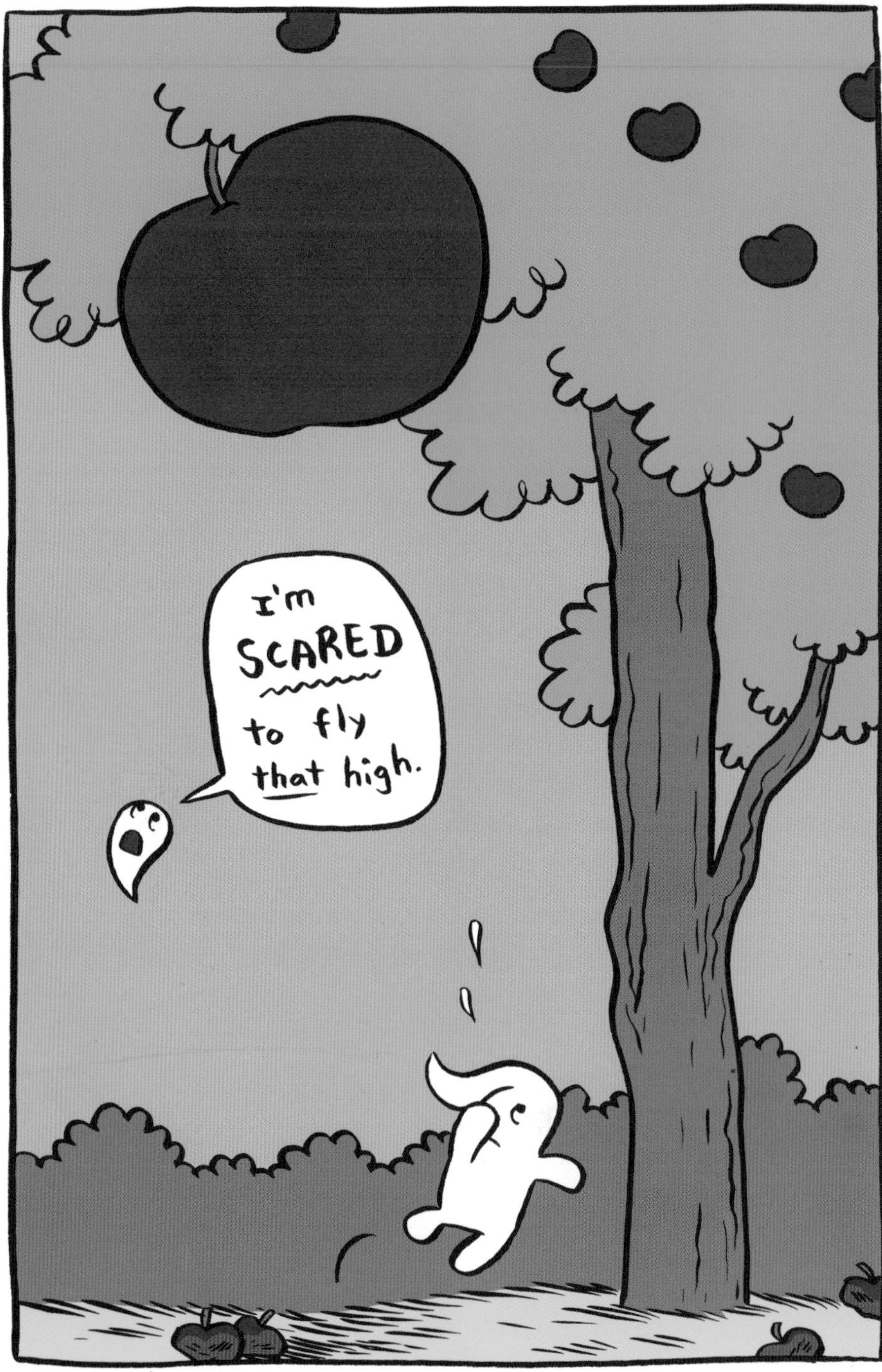
I'm SCARED to fly that high.

CHAPTER FIVE:

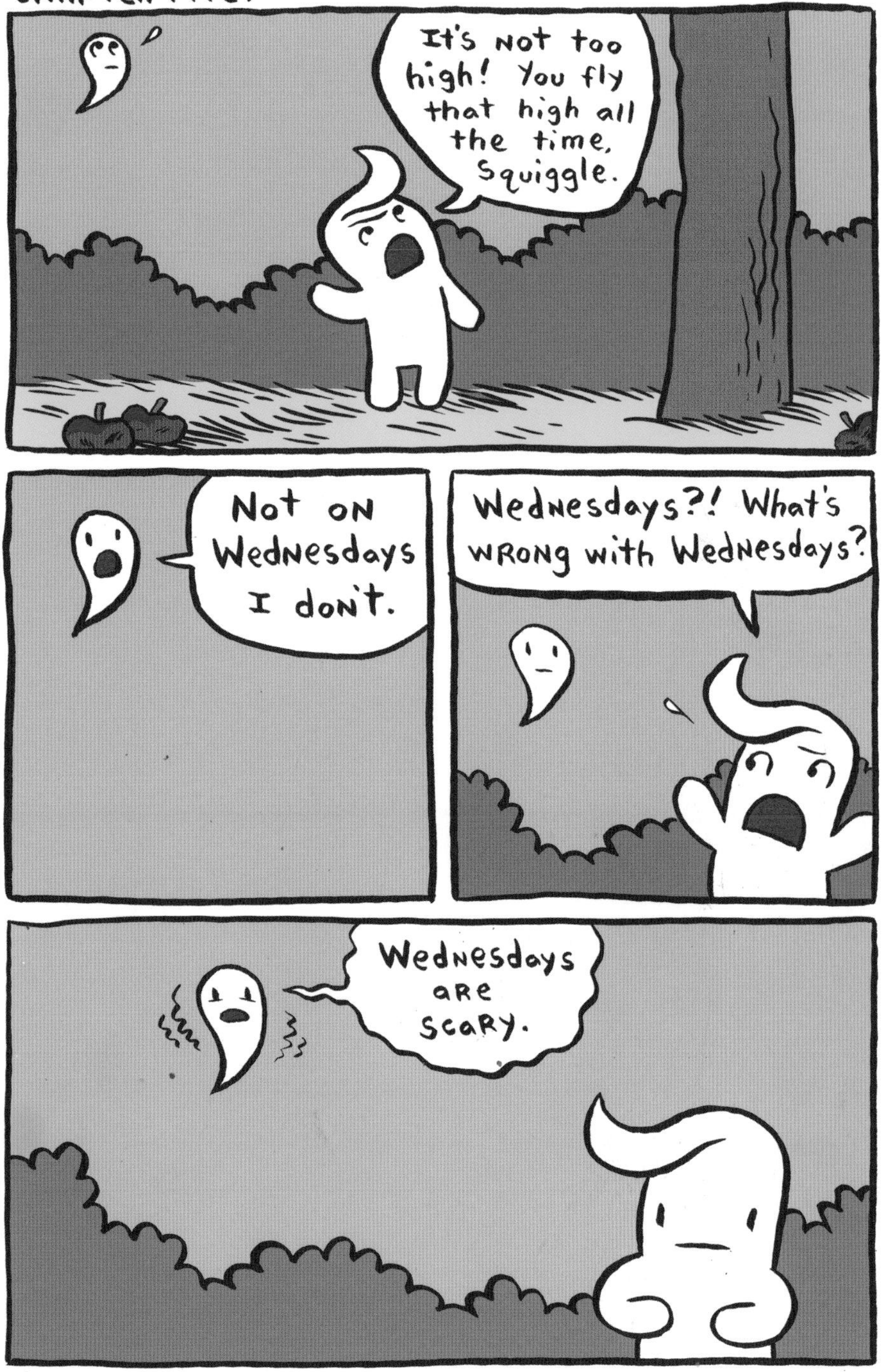
It's not too high! You fly that high all the time, Squiggle.
Not on Wednesdays I don't.
Wednesdays?! What's wrong with Wednesdays?
Wednesdays are scary.

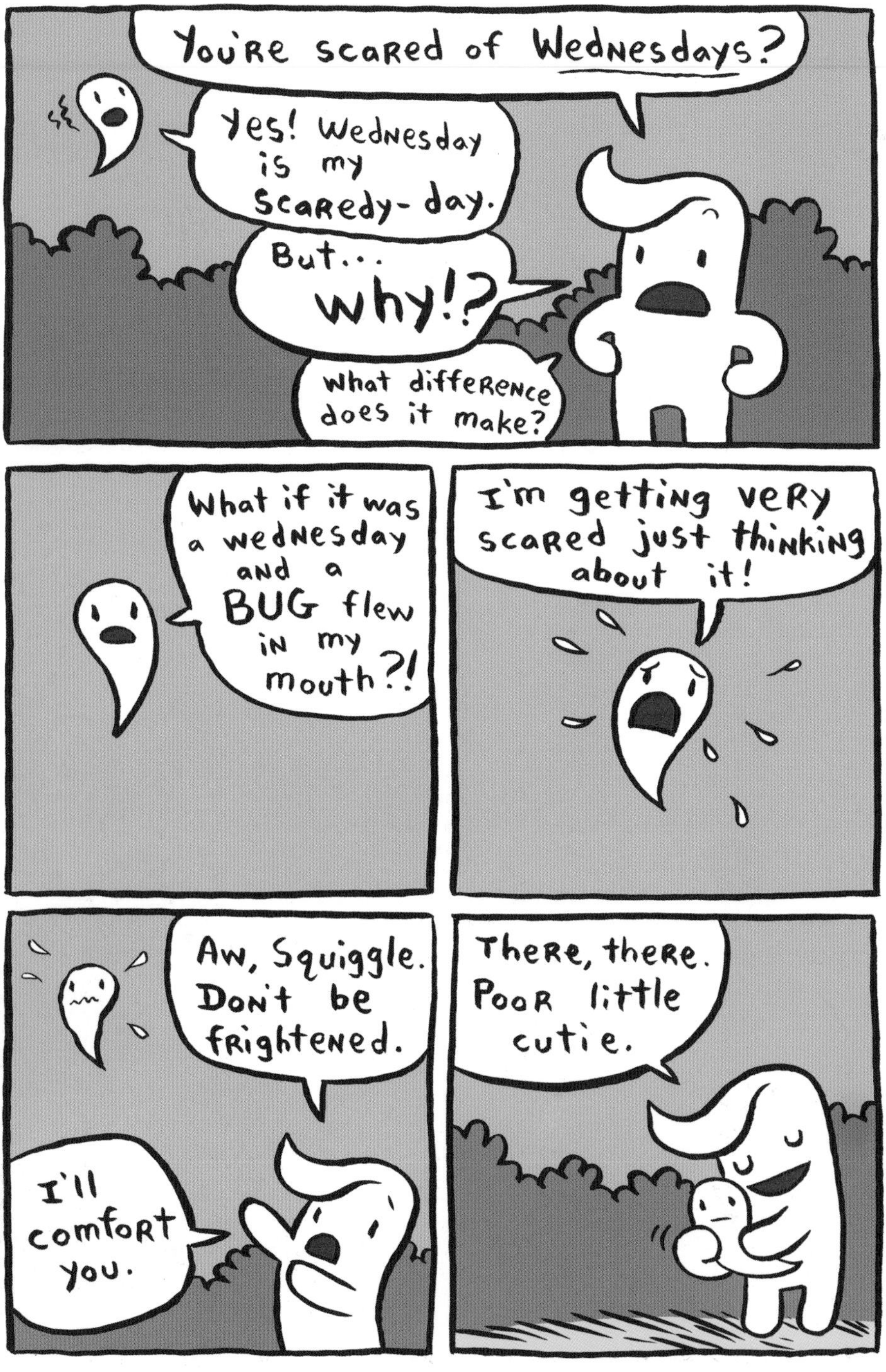
You're scared of Wednesdays?
Yes! Wednesday is my scaredy-day.
But... why!?
What difference does it make?
What if it was a wednesday and a BUG flew in my mouth?!
I'm getting VERY scared just thinking about it!
Aw, Squiggle. Don't be frightened.
I'll comfort you.
There, there. Poor little cutie.

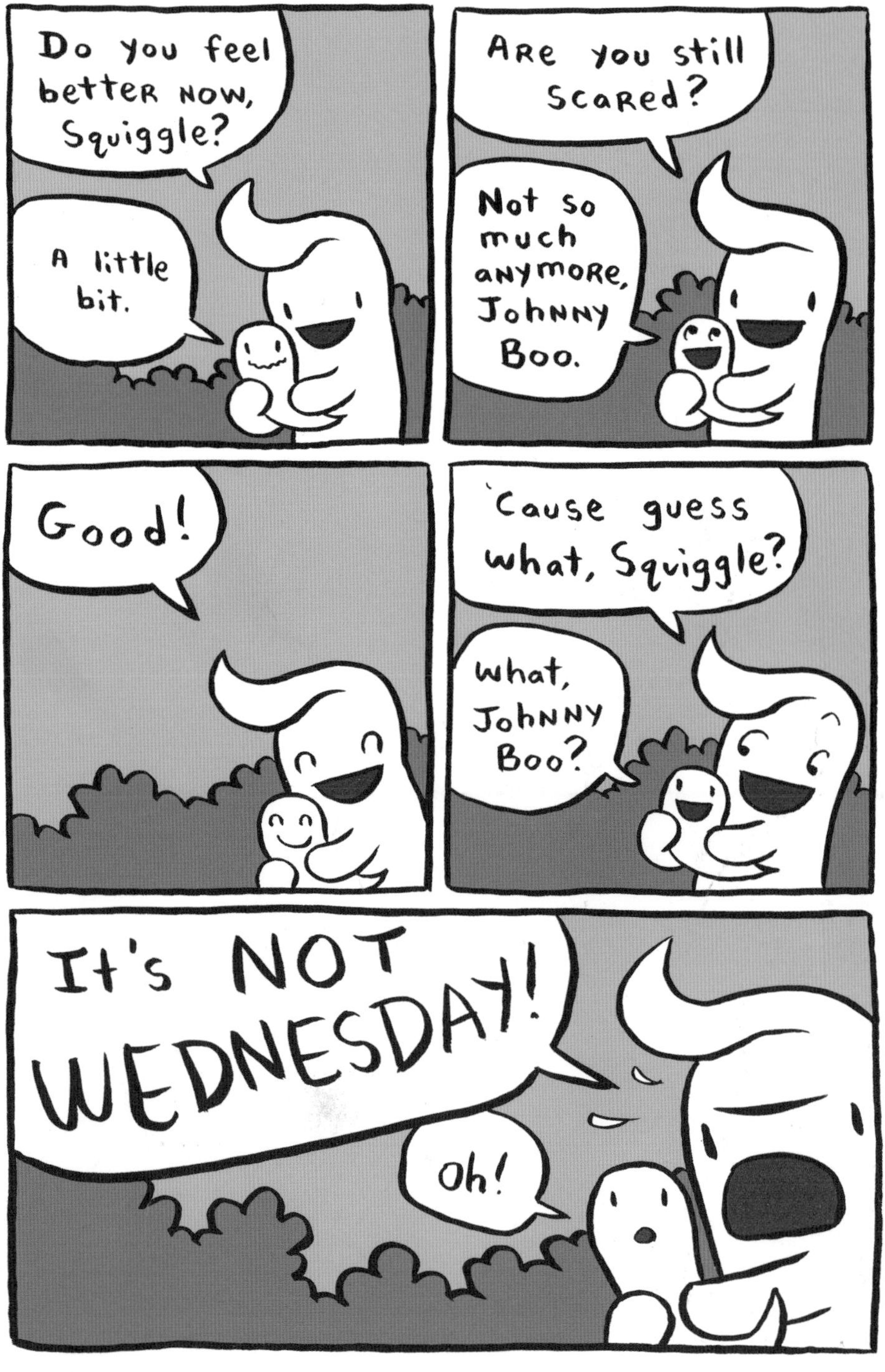
Do you feel better now, Squiggle?
A little bit.
Are you still scared?
Not so much anymore, Johnny Boo.
Good!
'Cause guess what, Squiggle?
What, Johnny Boo?
It's NOT WEDNESDAY!
Oh!

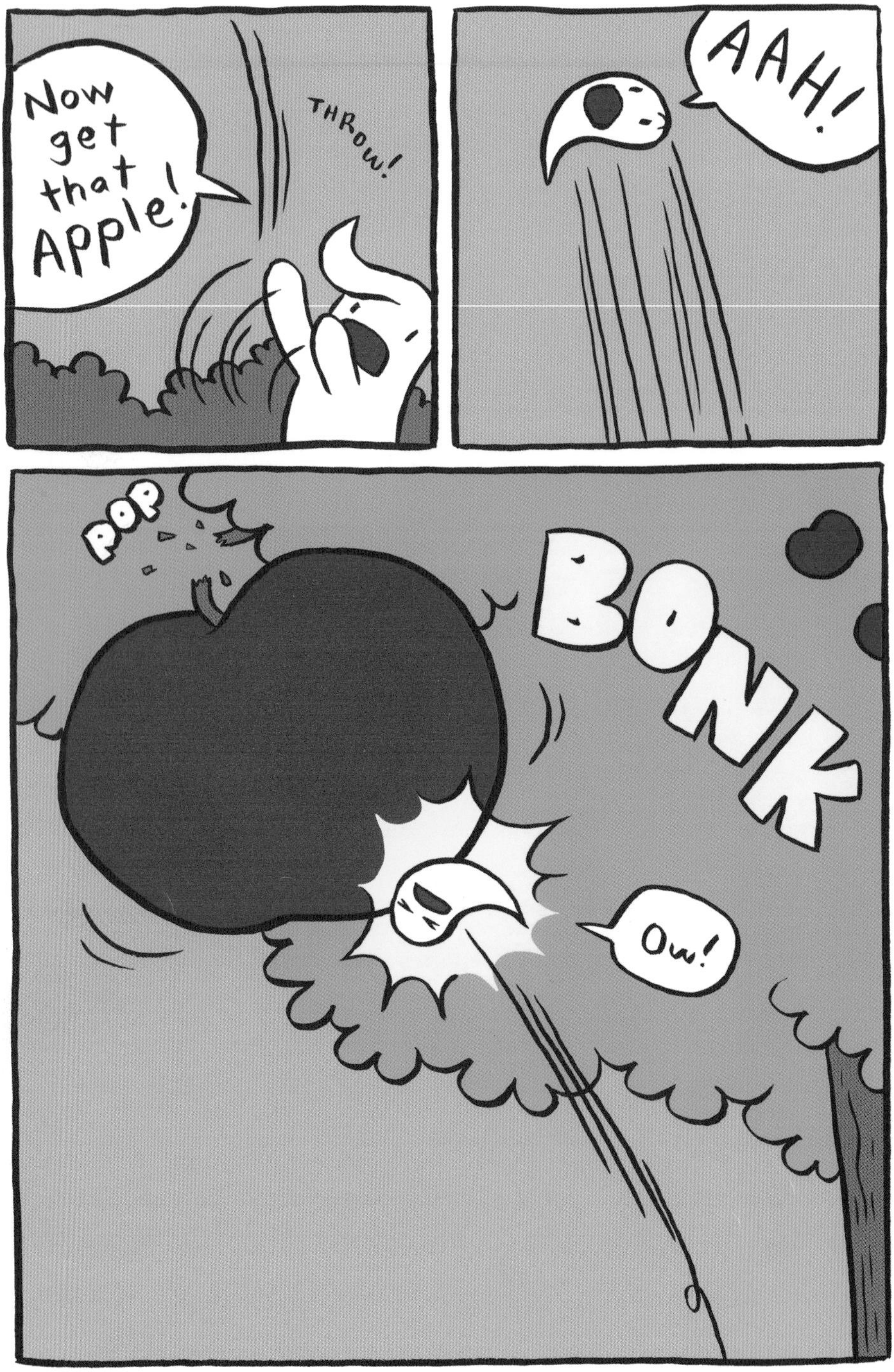
Now get that Apple!
THROW!
AAH!
POP
BONK
Ow!

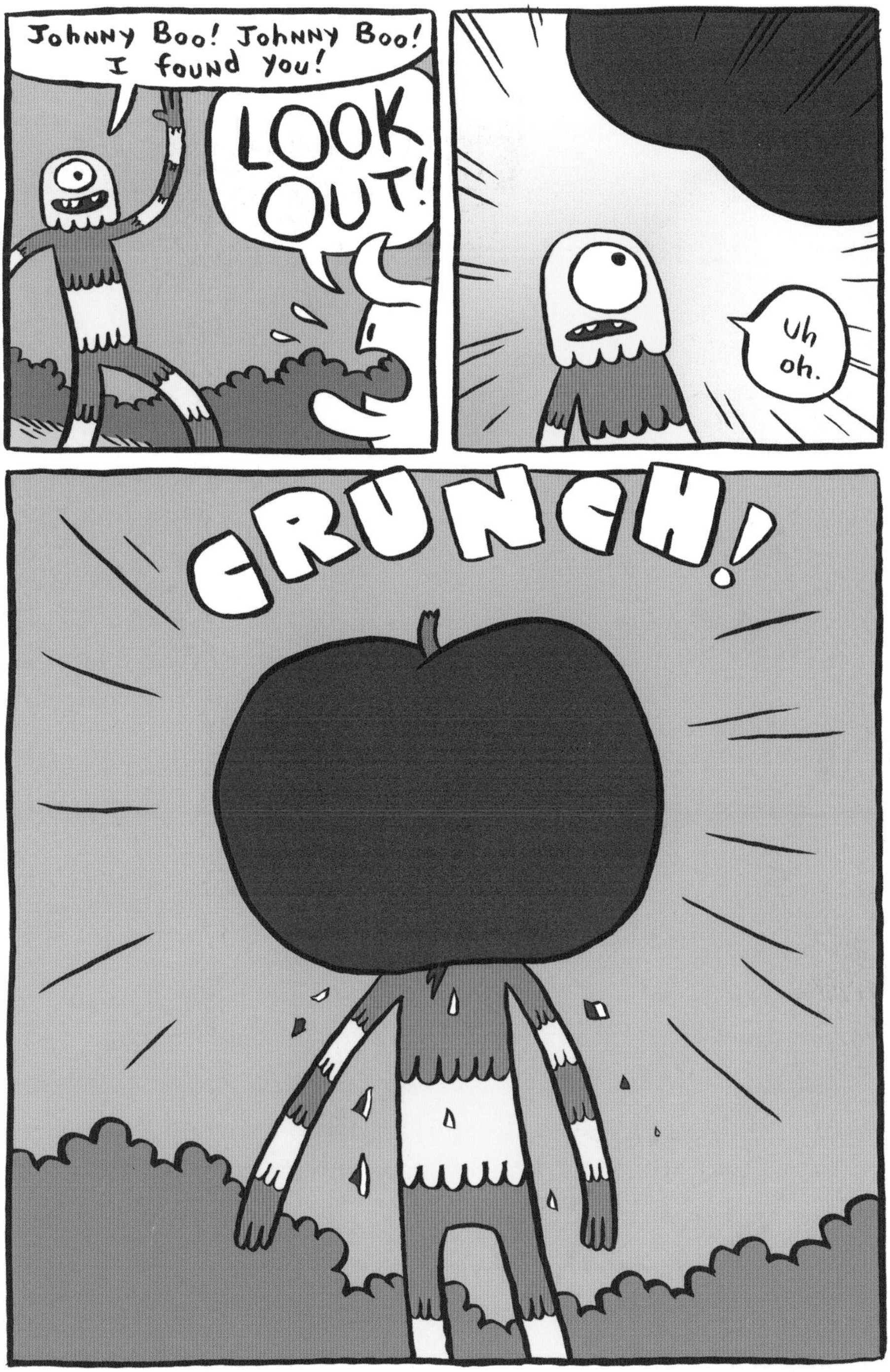
Johnny Boo! Johnny Boo! I found you!
LOOK OUT!
Uh oh.
CRUNCH!

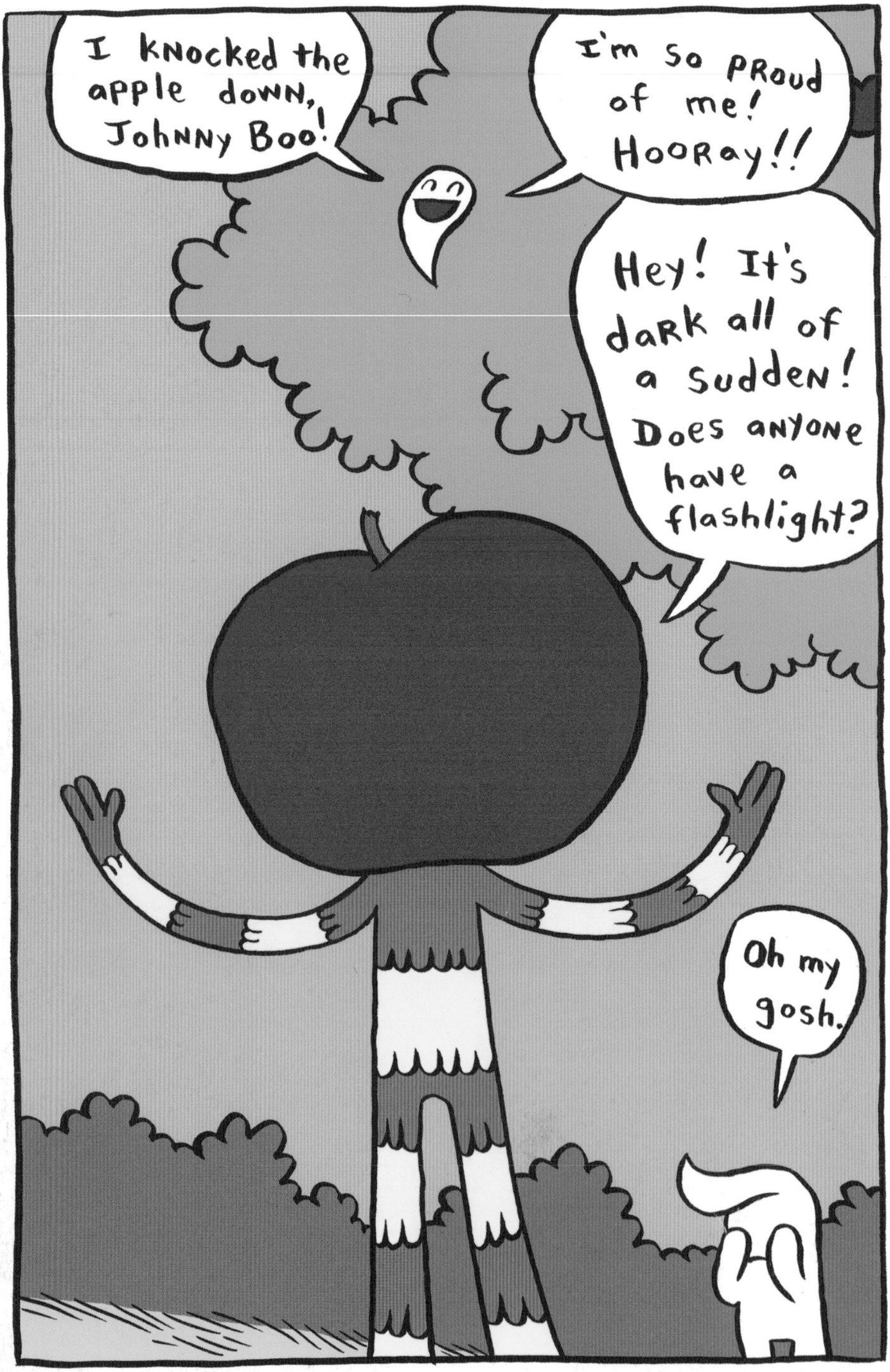
I knocked the apple down, Johnny Boo!
I'm so proud of me! Hooray!!
Hey! It's dark all of a sudden! Does anyone have a flashlight?
Oh my gosh.

CHAPTER SIX:

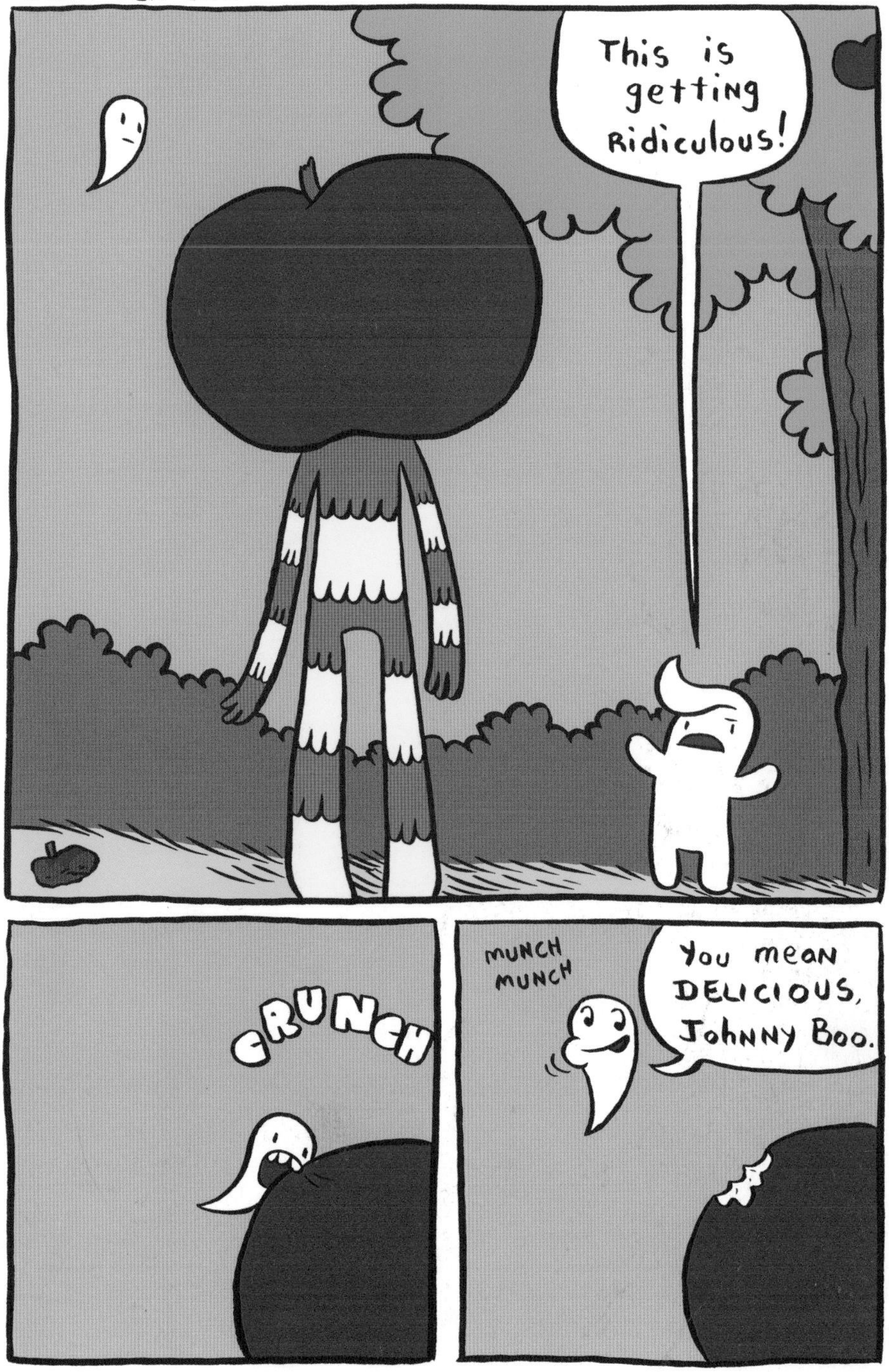
This is getting Ridiculous!
CRUNCH
MUNCH MUNCH
You mean DELICIOUS, Johnny Boo.

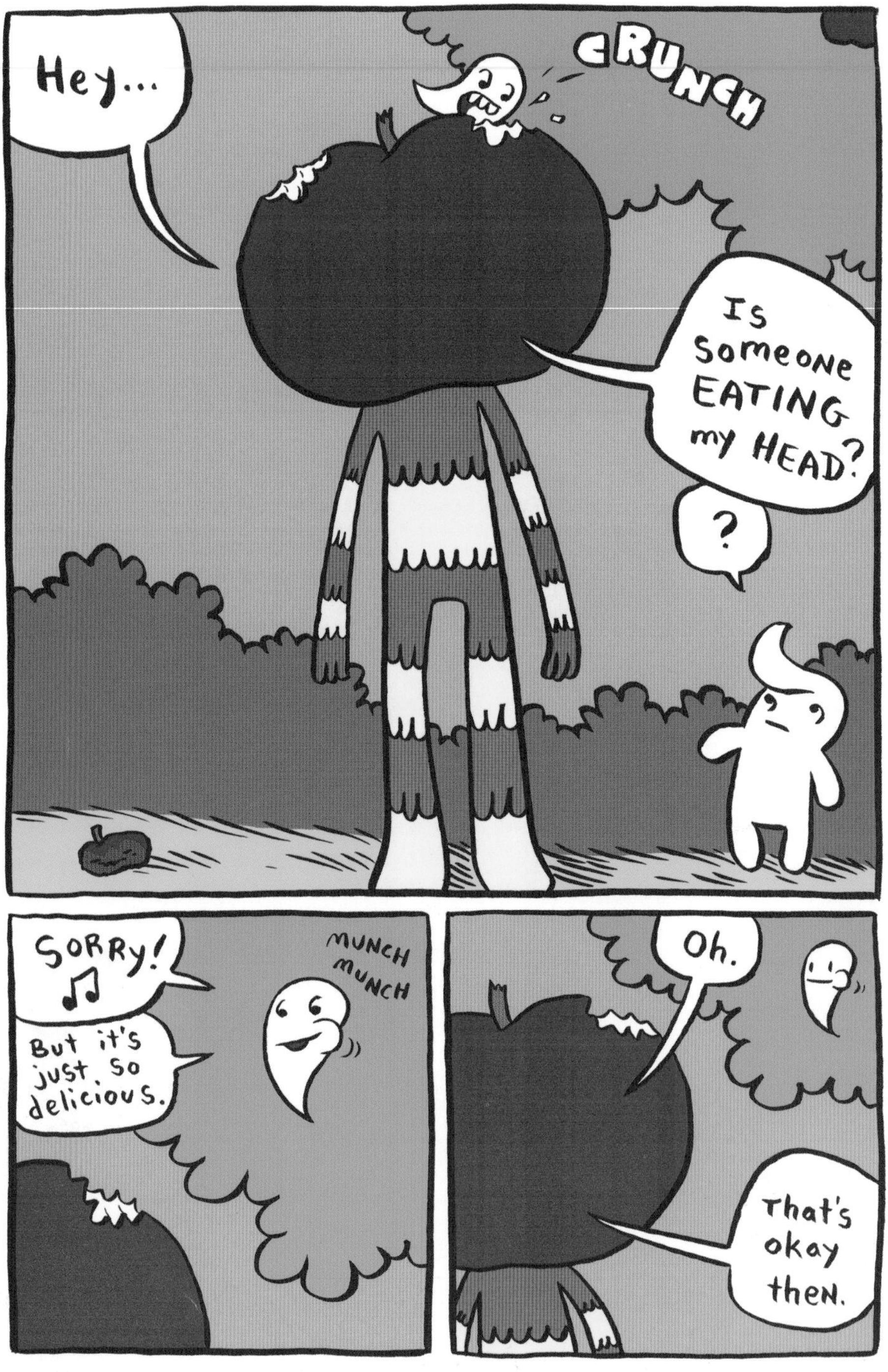
Hey...
CRUNCH
Is someone EATING my HEAD?
?
SORRY!
But it's just so delicious.
MUNCH MUNCH
Oh.
That's okay then.

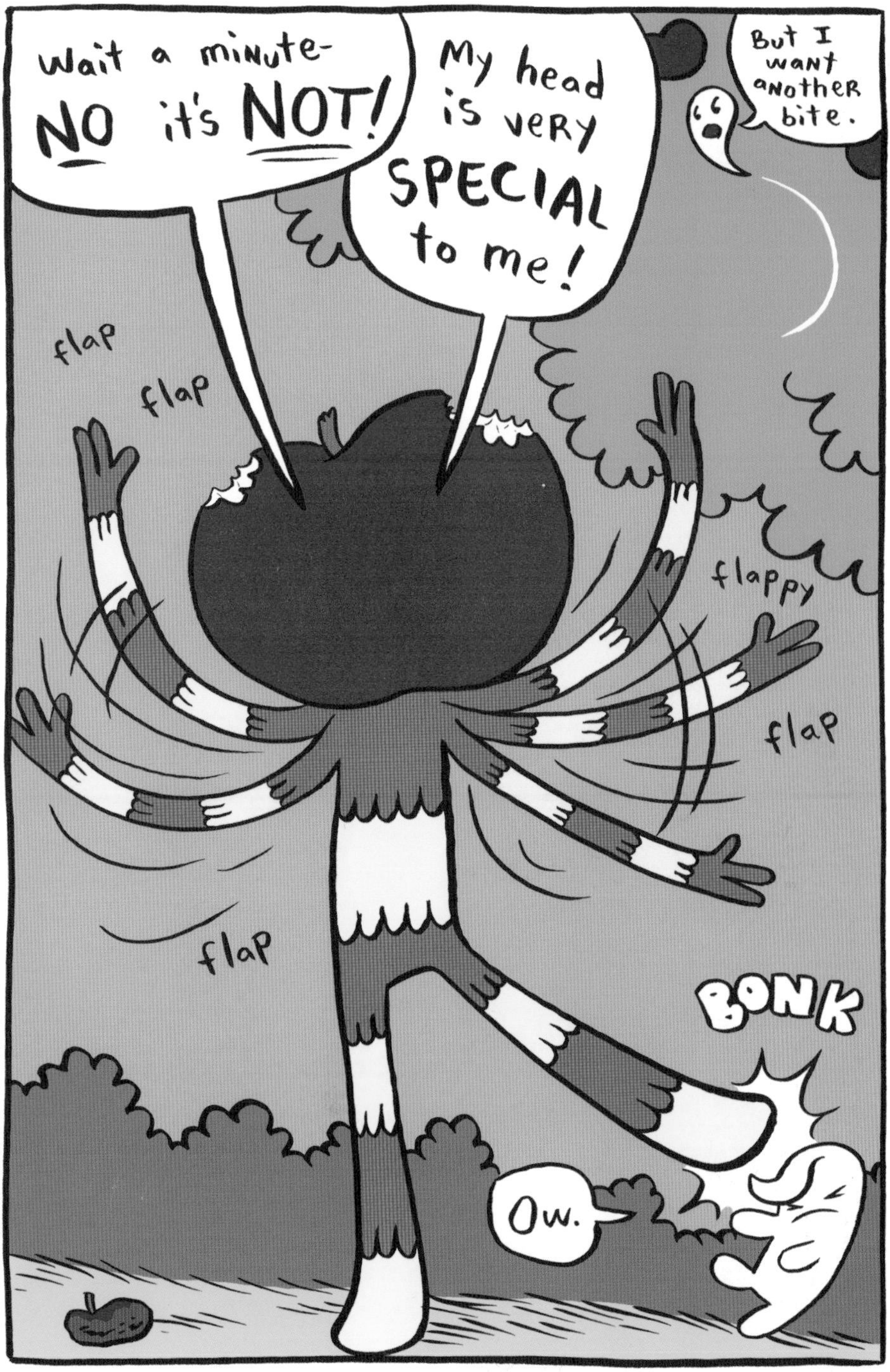
Wait a minute-
NO it's NOT!
My head is very SPECIAL to me!
But I want another bite.
flap
flap
flappy
flap
flap
BONK
Ow.

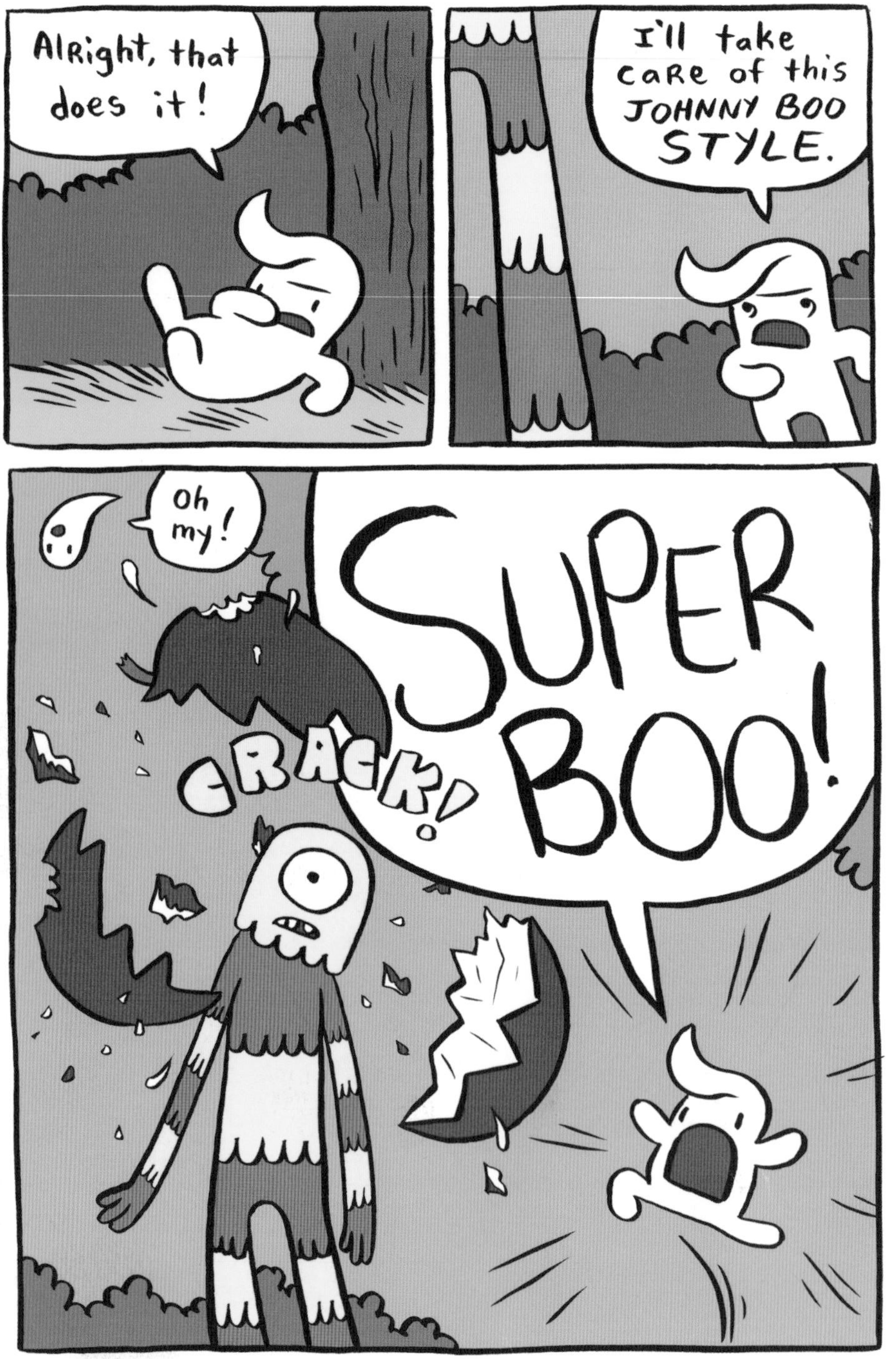
Alright, that does it!
I'll take care of this JOHNNY BOO STYLE.
Oh my!
SUPER BOO!
CRACK!

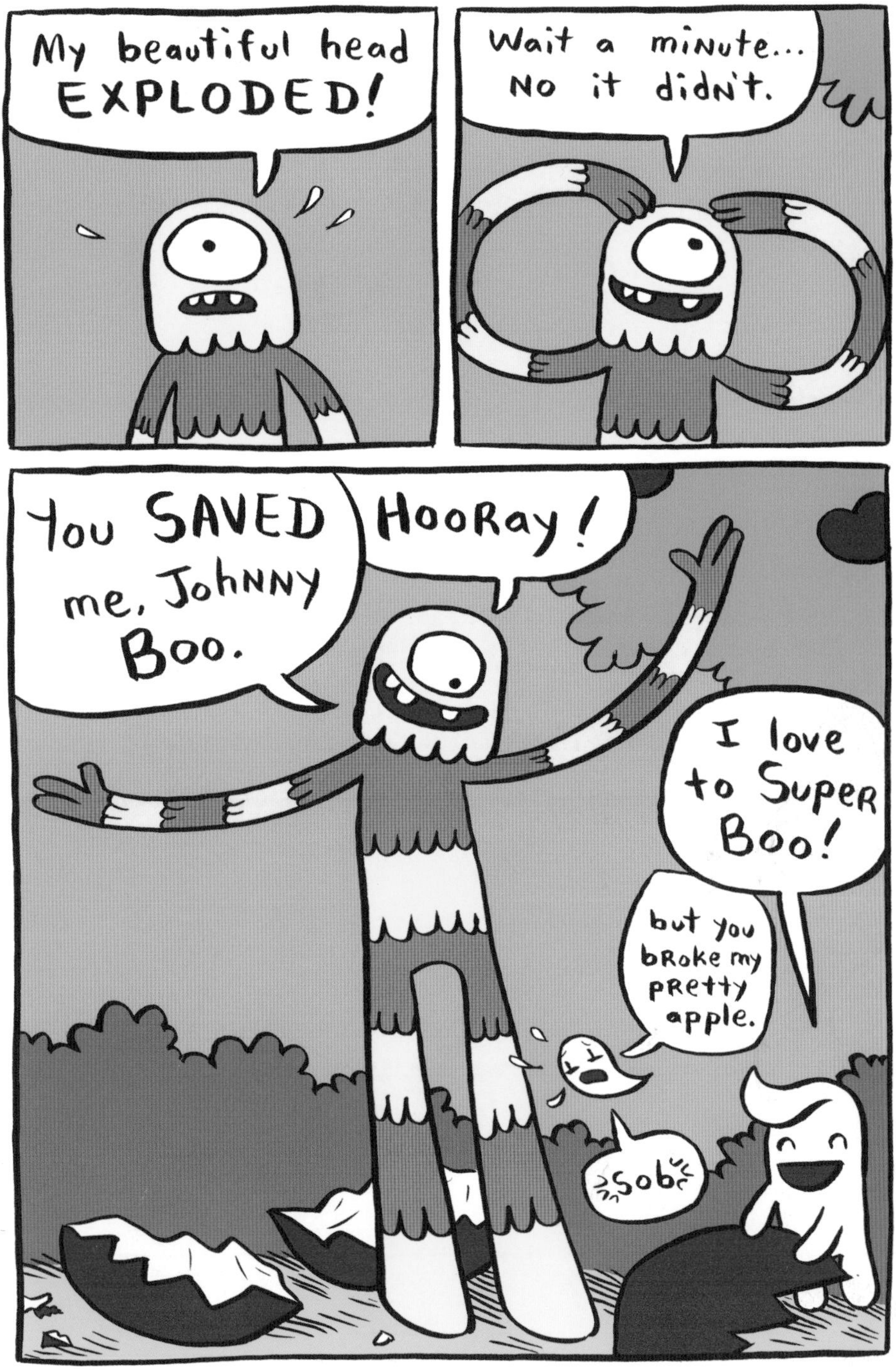
My beautiful head EXPLODED!
Wait a minute... No it didn't.
You SAVED me, Johnny Boo.
Hooray!
I love to Super Boo!
but you broke my pretty apple.
Sob

CHAPTER SEVEN:

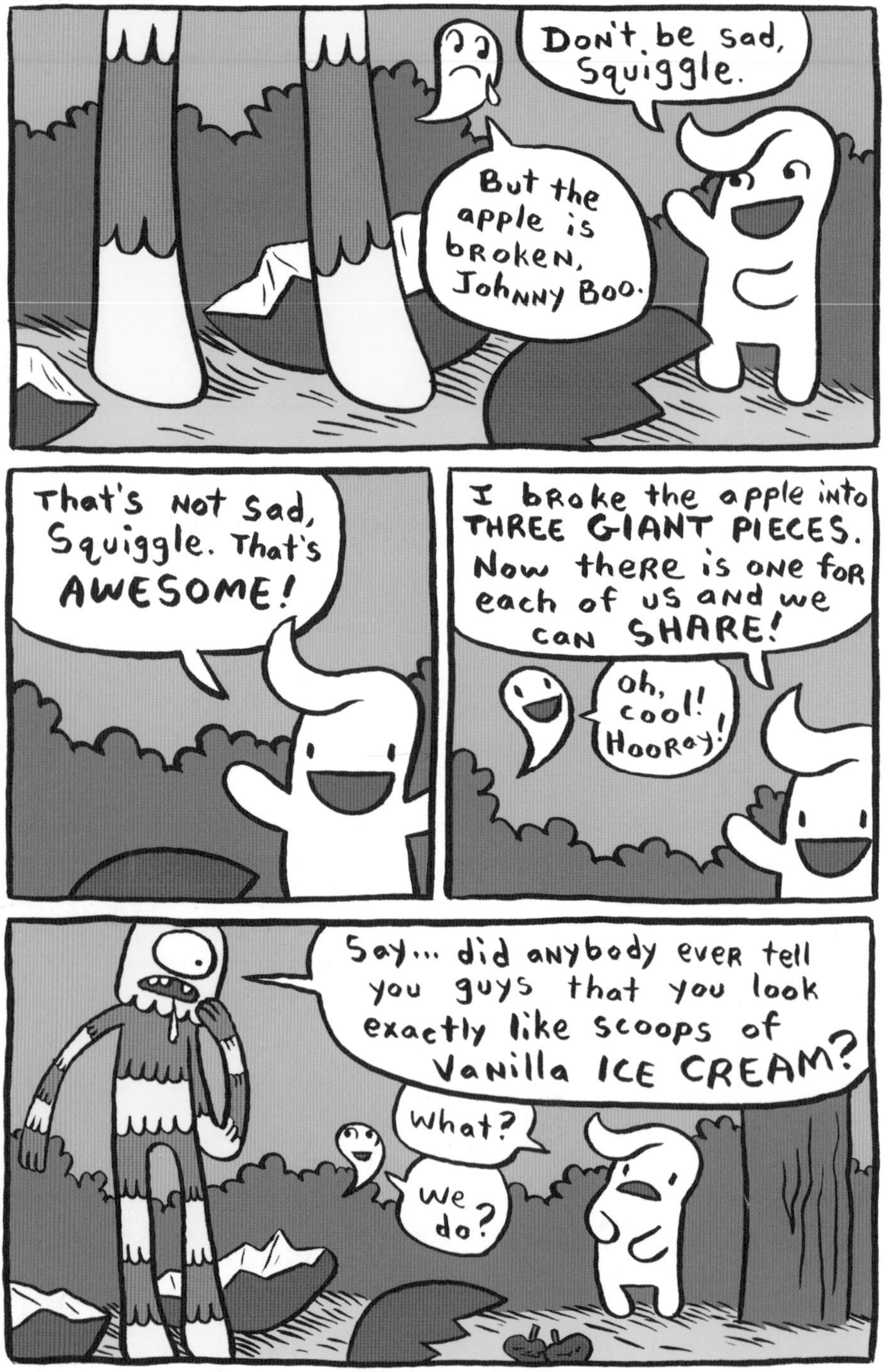

Don't be sad, Squiggle.
But the apple is broken, Johnny Boo.
That's not sad, Squiggle. That's AWESOME!
I broke the apple into THREE GIANT PIECES. Now there is one for each of us and we can SHARE!
Oh, cool! Hooray!
Say... did anybody ever tell you guys that you look exactly like scoops of Vanilla ICE CREAM?
What?
We do?

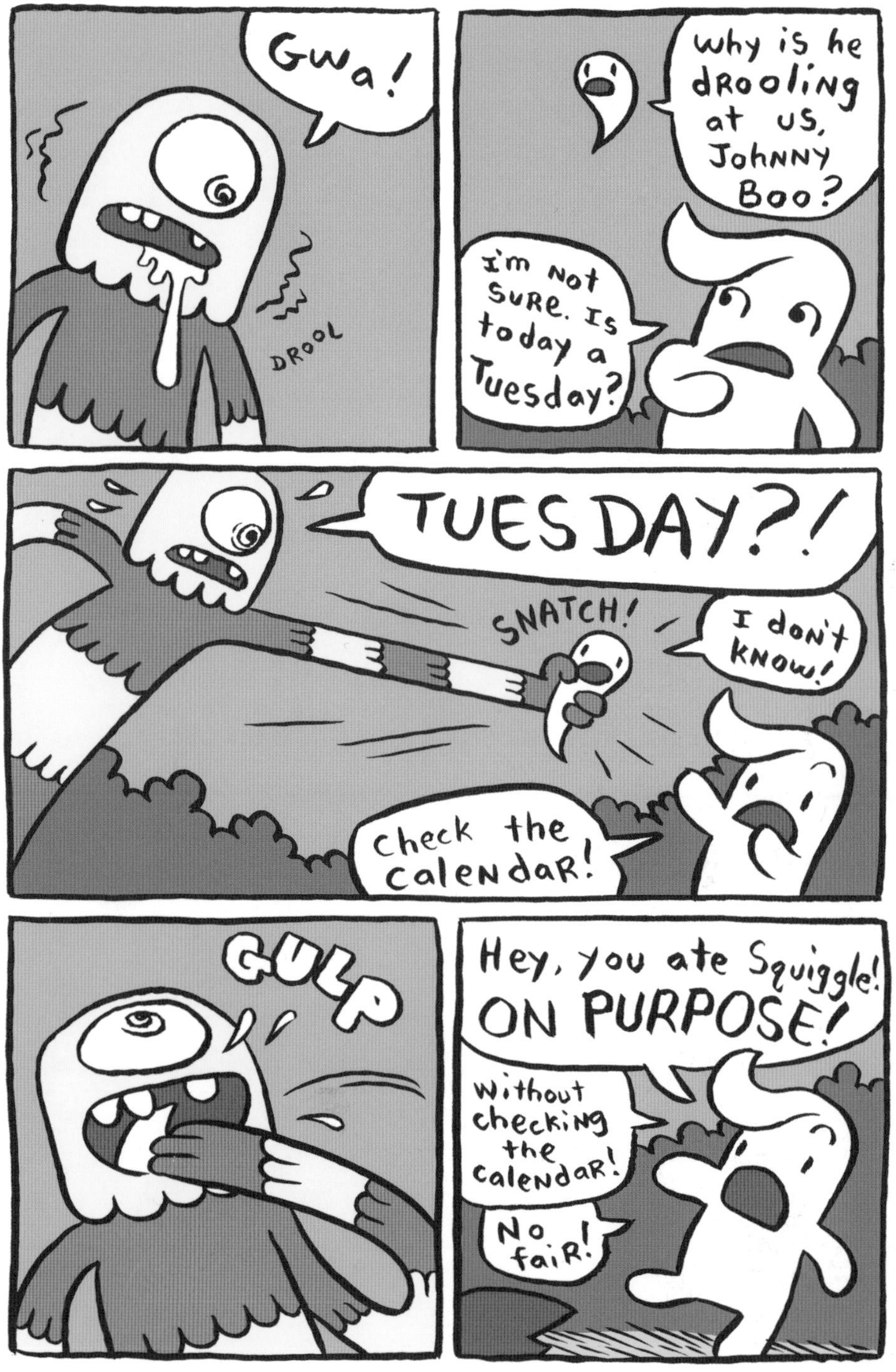
Gwa!
DROOL
why is he drooling at us, Johnny Boo?
I'm not sure. Is today a Tuesday?
TUESDAY?!
SNATCH!
I don't know!
Check the calendar!
GULP
Hey, you ate Squiggle! ON PURPOSE!
without checking the calendar!
No fair!

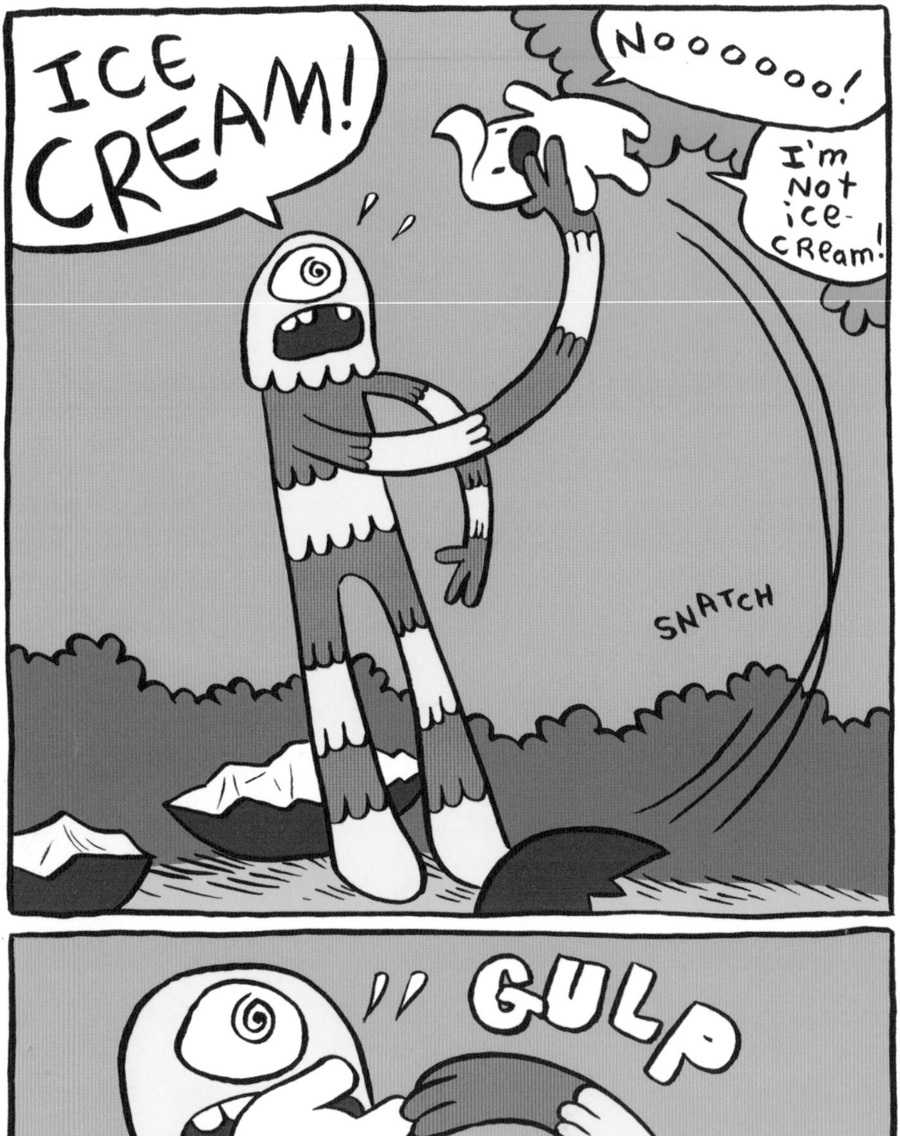
ICE CREAM!
Nooooooo!
I'm Not ice-cream!
SNATCH
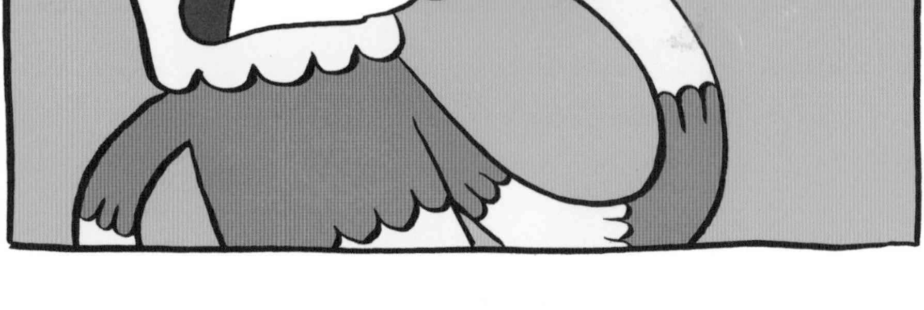
GULP

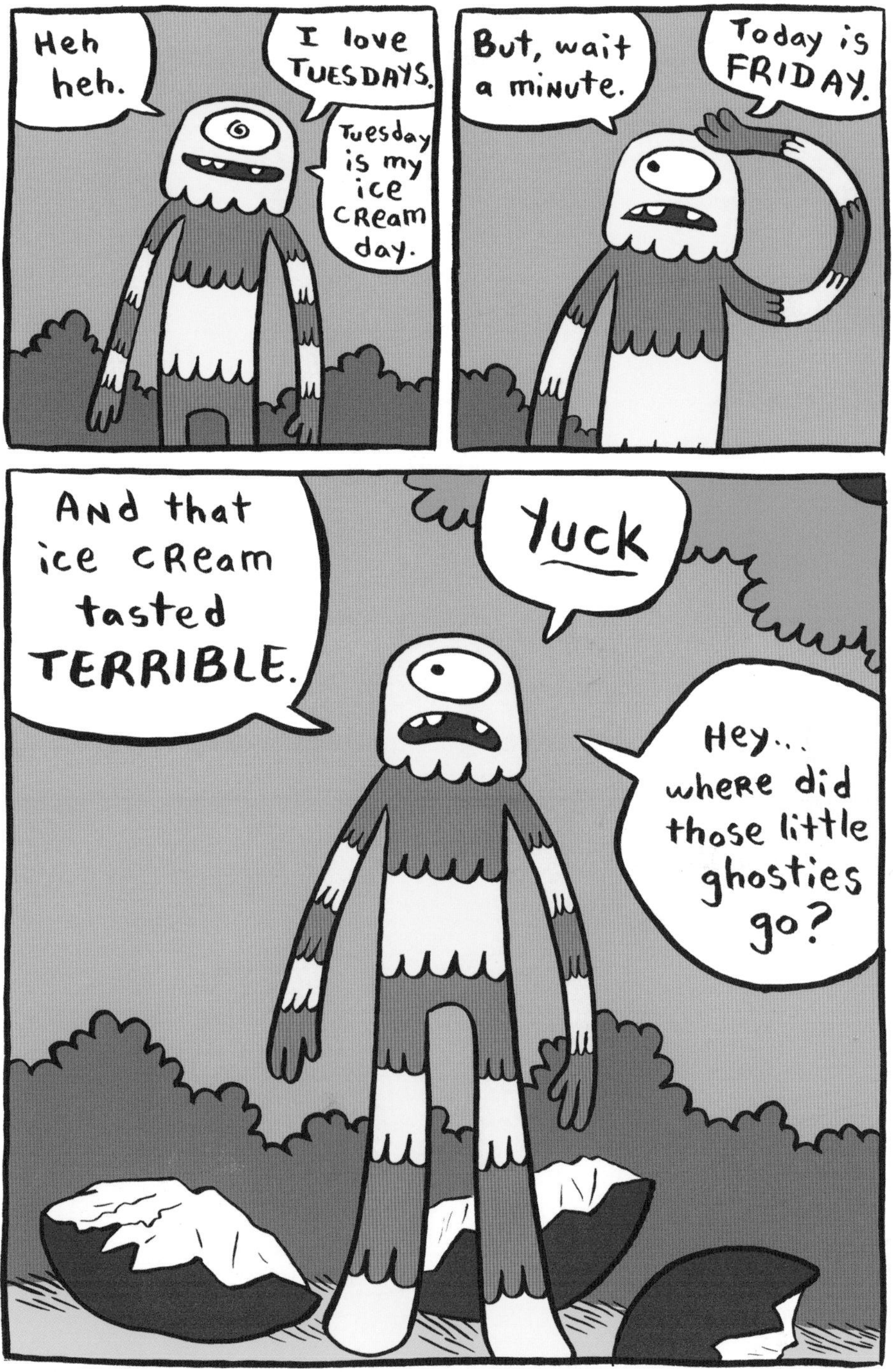
Heh heh.
I love TUESDAYS.
Tuesday is my ice cream day.
But, wait a minute.
Today is FRIDAY.
And that ice cream tasted TERRIBLE.
Yuck
Hey... where did those little ghosties go?

CHAPTER EIGHT:

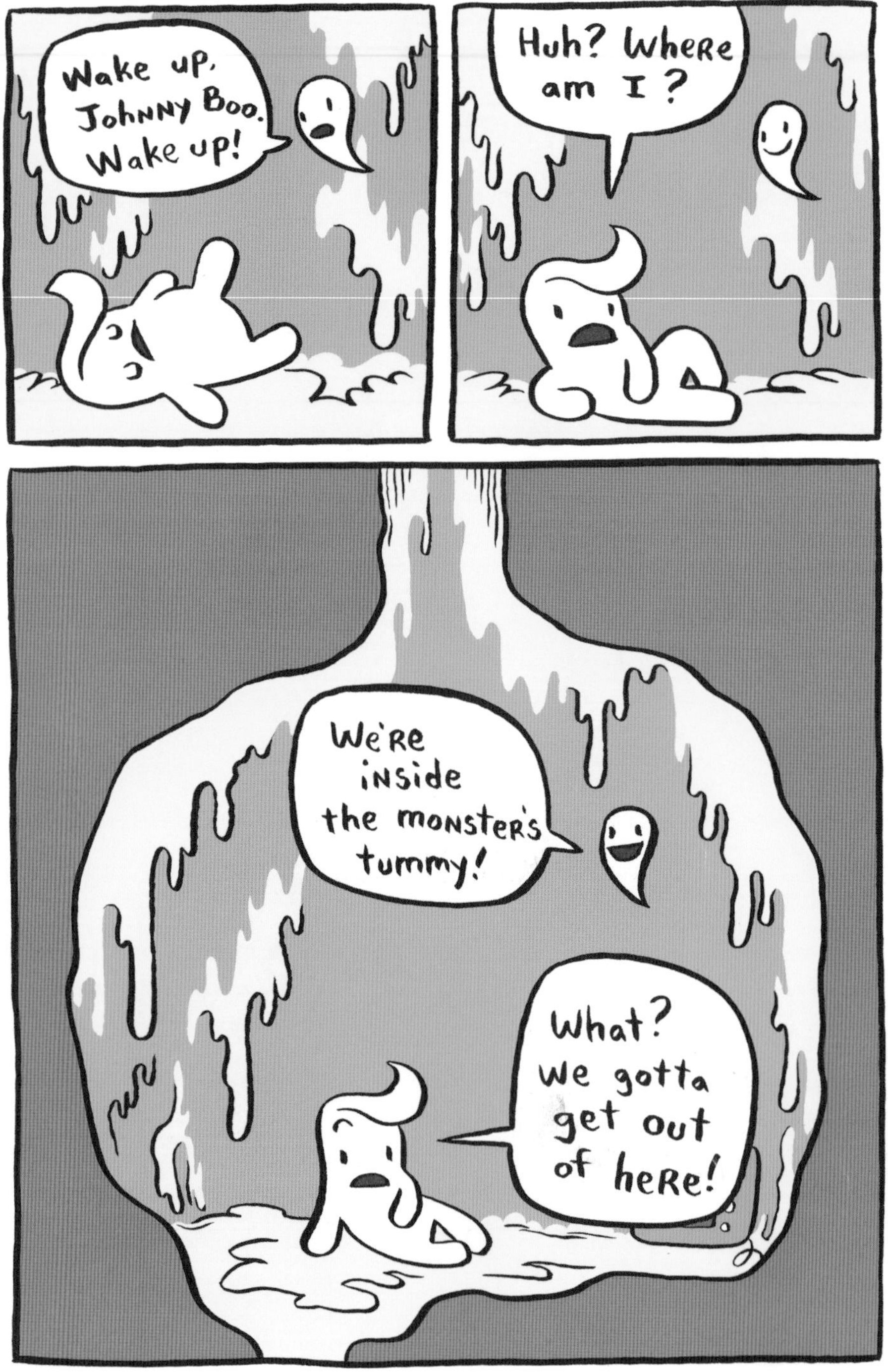
Wake up, Johnny Boo. Wake up!
Huh? Where am I?
We're inside the monster's tummy!
What? We gotta get out of here!

Activate your Squiggle Power RIGHT AWAY!

HURRY!

Make him burp us up.

Relax, Johnny Boo. Take it easy.

But I'm too cute to be digested!

It takes hours for the stomach to digest a meal, Johnny Boo. There's no rush.

Oh.

Hey, how come there's so much room in here?

Monsters have magic tummies. Plus, look at this.

His tummy has television!

37

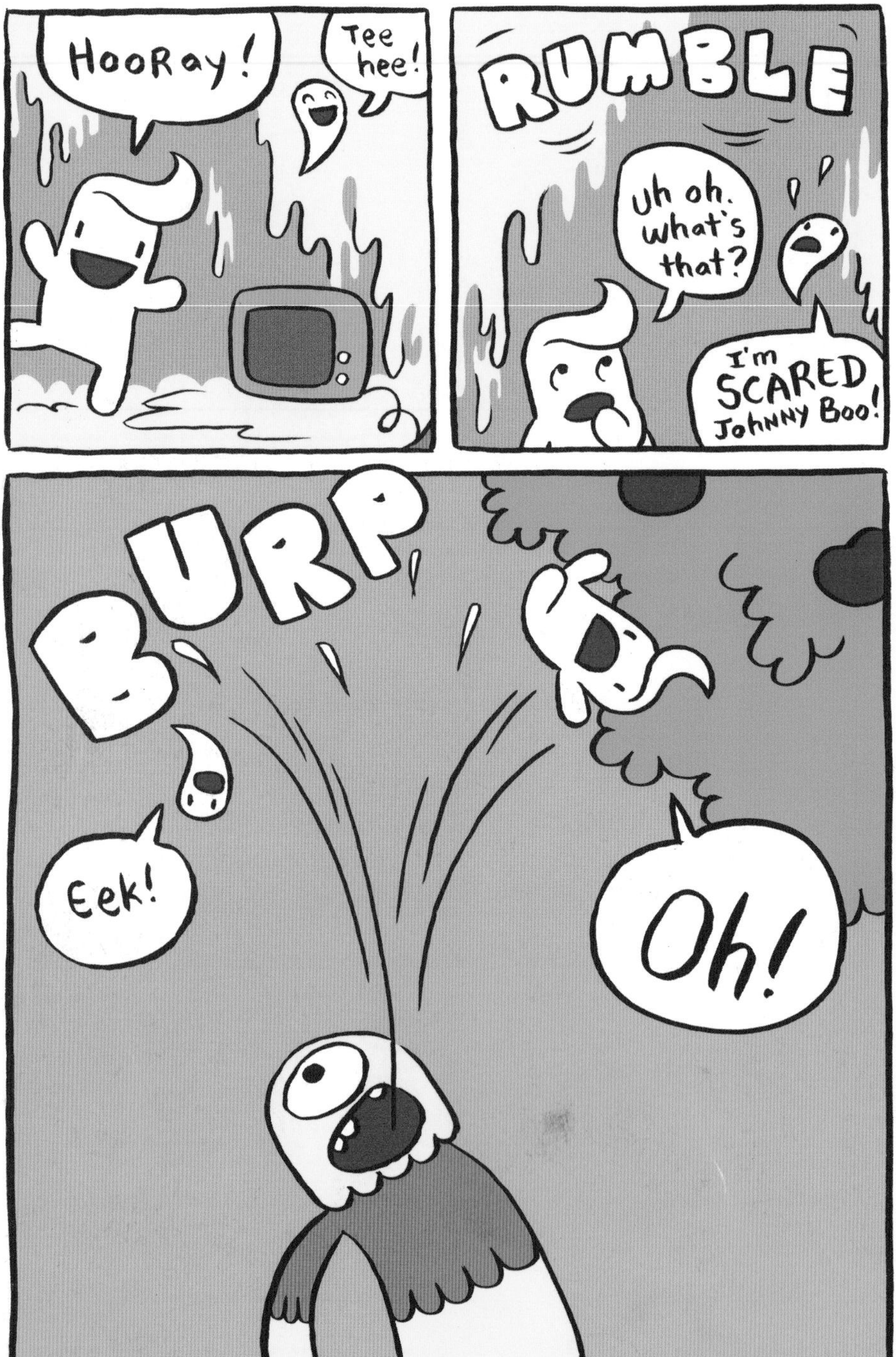
HooRay!
Tee hee!
RUMBLE
uh oh. what's that?
I'm SCARED Johnny Boo!
BURP
Eek!
Oh!

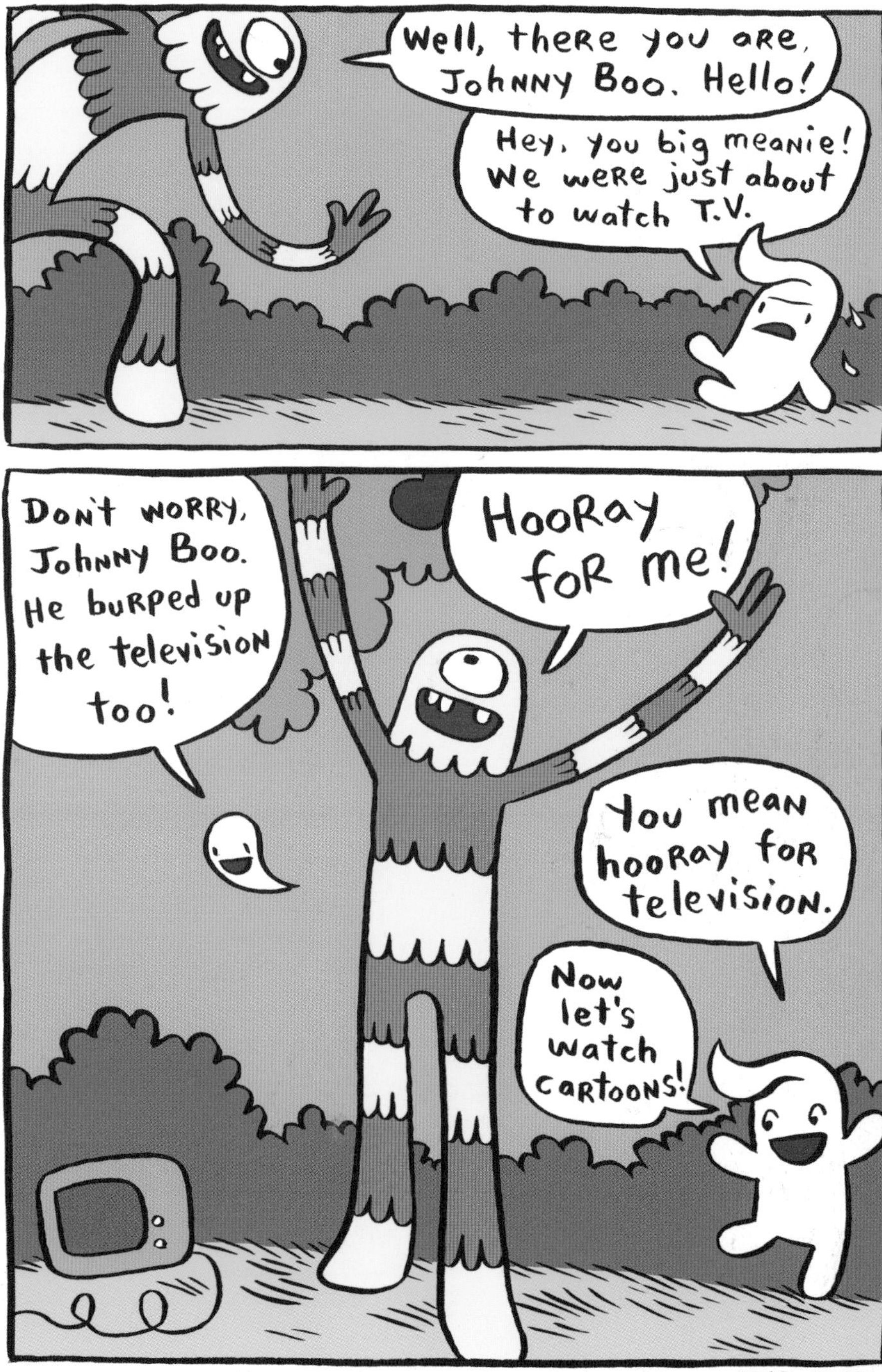
Well, there you are, Johnny Boo. Hello!
Hey, you big meanie! We were just about to watch T.V.
Don't worry, Johnny Boo. He burped up the television too!
Hooray for me!
You mean hooray for television.
Now let's watch cartoons!

THE END

A PHOTO OF THE AUTHOR:

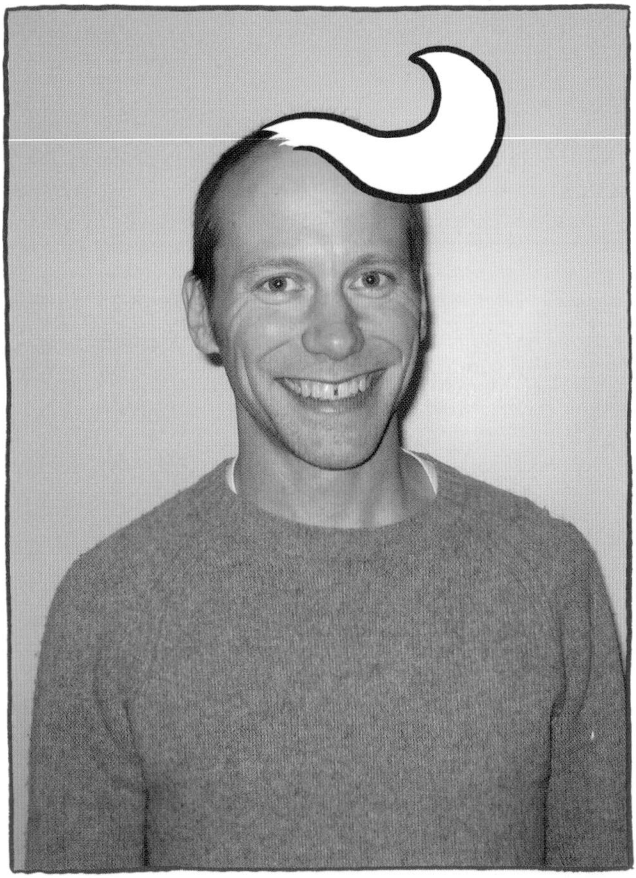